I Am America

UNITED TO STRIKE

◆

A Story of the Delano Grape Workers

Book design by Jake Slavik
Illustrations by Eric Freeberg

Consultant: L. MSP Burns, Associate Professor in Asian American Studies, UCLA

Photographs ©: Library of Congress, 157 (top); George Ballis/Take Stock/The Image Works, 157 (bottom)

Published in the United States by Jolly Fish Press, an imprint of North Star Editions, Inc.

First Edition
First Printing, 2019

Library of Congress Cataloging-in-Publication Data
Names: Zenk, Molly, 1978- author. | Freeberg, Eric, illustrator.
Title: United to strike : a story of the Delano Grape workers / by Molly Zenk ; illustrated by Eric Freeberg.
Description: Heights, MN : Jolly Fish Press, [2020] | Series: I am America | Summary: "The Delano Grape Strike brings Filipino and Mexican farmworkers together, but threatens Tala Mendoza's relationship with her best friend" —Provided by publisher.
Identifiers: LCCN 2018038114 (print) | LCCN 2018041145 (ebook) | ISBN 9781631632853 (e-book) | ISBN 9781631632846 (pbk.) | ISBN 9781631632839 (hardcover)
Subjects: | CYAC: Best friends—Fiction. | Friendship—Fiction. | Agricultural laborers—Fiction. | Grape Strike, Calif. 1965-1970—Fiction. | Chavez, Cesar, 1927-1993—Fiction. | United Farm Workers—Fiction. | Family life—California—Fiction. | Investigative reporting—Fiction. | Filipino Americans—Fiction. | Mexican Americans—Fiction. | California—History—20th century—Fiction.
Classification: LCC PZ7.1.Z45 (ebook) | LCC PZ7.1.Z45 Un 2019 (print) | DDC [Fic]—dc23
LC record available at https://lccn.loc.gov/2018038114

Jolly Fish Press
North Star Editions, Inc.
2297 Waters Drive
Mendota Heights, MN 55120
www.jollyfishpress.com

I Am America

UNITED TO STRIKE

A Story of the Delano Grape Workers

By Molly Zenk

Illustrated by Eric Freeberg

JOLLY
FiSH
PRESS

Mendota Heights, Minnesota

Terms

adyos – Goodbye in Tagalog

AWOC – Agricultural Workers Organizing Committee. In 1965 the AWOC in Delano was made up of mostly Filipinos and led by Larry Itliong.

bracero – A Mexican worker/laborer from Mexico. Not the same as Mexican American.

hay naku – No direct translation but is the Tagalog equivalent of "oh my!" or "geez!"

hola – Hello in Spanish

huelga – Strike in Spanish

kare-kare – Traditional Filipino stew with vegetables, oxtail, and peanut sauce

lola – Grandmother in Tagalog

lumpia – Traditional Filipino spring roll

manong – The word for elder or older brother in Tagalog. Historically, manongs were part of the first wave of Filipino immigrants to the United States.

nanay – Mother in Tagalog

nene – Little girl in Tagalog

NFWA – National Farm Workers Association. The NFWA was started by Chicano farmworker César Chávez in 1962.

oyab – Sweetheart in Tagalog

tatay – Father in Tagalog

UFW – United Farm Workers. AWOC and NFWA merged in the summer of 1966 to become the United Farm Workers Organizing Committee, also known as UFWOC, or just UFW.

yema – Filipino candy made from condensed milk and egg yolks

PART I
Fall 1965

Chapter One

September 1, 1965
Dear Diary,

Today I am eleven. It's funny because I don't feel eleven. I still feel ten, but somehow, waking up this morning makes me a whole year older. My best friend Jasmine says being eleven makes us closer to God. I don't know if she means that we're one year closer to death or just that it's our church confirmation year. Jasmine is morbid (my new word of the day) so it could go either way. "Think happy thoughts" and Jasmine don't go hand in hand. It's more like "prepare for the worst." Maybe she thinks in the temporary instead of the permanent because her dad and grandparents used to be migrants. They traveled from farm to farm looking for work. When they got here, the work stuck around so they stuck around. Jasmine still thinks that can change, for some reason. She doesn't listen when I tell her my lola says the vineyard work in Delano has been steady for generations.

"Things change," Jasmine insists. "Things always change."

"Things can stay the same too," I remind her.

I guess Jasmine doesn't believe in the power of positive thinking. I don't know if I do either, but I do believe that words are powerful. I like words. There's just something about them—the flow, the music—that makes me want to write them all down. They're always whirling around like a crop duster airplane propeller, waiting to be plucked out and put down on paper. I even went to our library after school and looked up all the jobs you can do with just words. No labor—unless you count what's going on in your head—and no moving around so much, like Jasmine's family used to do before they got to Delano.

It turns out there are a lot of jobs that I could do with words. My favorite is "investigative reporter." I like the sound of that. "Tala Mendoza, investigative reporter." It sounds official and important, doesn't it? If I was an investigative reporter, I'd be taken seriously all the time. People would talk to me instead of just smiling and saying "Well, aren't you the cutest thing ever . . . have a yema." I like yema as well as the next person, but I don't want to have one shoved at me anytime I try to do something serious.

Jasmine's brother Isko, who I don't like because he's thirteen and thinks he knows everything about everything, says if I write more, maybe I'll talk less. Is it my fault that I have all these words that need to come out? Isko bought me and Jasmine each a diary for our birthdays. He says it's to get us to stop chattering like magpies. It makes sense that he'd give Jasmine a present because she's his sister. But it's weird that he got me one too. Before now, I think the most Isko has ever given me is a punch in the arm. Nanay is practically planning our wedding now. She says Isko buying me a gift "means something." I'd rather marry the Creature from The Black Lagoon than Isko, but I didn't tell Nanay that. It would burst her bubble. Let her plan if it makes her happy. A happy Nanay is the best birthday present of all.

Jasmine has five older brothers and two younger sisters. I have zero brothers and zero sisters but that's not because Nanay and Tatay didn't want a big family like the Perezes. Nanay and Tatay always wanted more kids, but I'm their only treasure on earth.

Nanay said she needed an extra-special name for their extra-special girl. She says she took one look at my face and named me Tala after the goddess of the morning and evening star. Goddess Tala's love stretches all the way to the sun and moon and back. Nanay's love for me did the same when she first saw me. I don't mind being the only kid in my family. It's not lonely at all. Jasmine lives nearby and has enough brothers and sisters for everyone. In our little apartment, Lola lives with us and we have a lot of aunties and uncles coming and going depending on the season and which crop they're following. There always seems to be someone looking for a job on the ranch or just passing through on their way to the next harvest. Tatay says we're the landing place for wayward (yesterday's word of the day) family.

Sometimes I wonder where we would live if we didn't live in such an agricultural area. Sure, Delano is a nice enough place and great if you have a vineyard or want to work in one, but it's not all that exciting. Not that I'm dying for excitement or anything, but it would be nice if the town didn't feel so sleepy. Sometimes I think it (and me) needs a good shake to wake up. Last year, my teacher gave us an assignment to categorize buildings in town. Here's what I found:

churches: 28
elementary schools: 4
high schools: 1
hospitals: 1
newspapers: 1
banks: 4
movie theaters: 2
doctors: 8
dentists: 4
eye doctors: 4
bookstores: 0

My least favorite part of this list is the zero bookstores. An up-and-coming investigative reporter like me needs a bookstore or a public library. Tatay can't always take me the thirty miles to Bakersfield to get books, no matter how much I want him too.

Most families, like Jasmine's, live in town. They rent a little house on the west side of town and drive to the ranch. Three of her older brothers moved out to the single-men housing on the ranch, so the Perez house is less crowded than normal. In the men's housing, it's only four to a room and all meals are free. Well, not exactly free, but close. Isko says the boss takes the money out of your wages, but you still don't have to worry about cooking, so that's something, I guess. He plans to join his brothers in the men's housing as soon as he's old enough. I have bigger dreams than picking, girdling, and packing grapes. And that is Isko's problem. He doesn't know how to dream big.

Since there's only four of us in my family's house and we don't need all the space the Perezes do, we don't actually live in Delano. We live on the ranch just outside of Delano in an apartment. Actually, it's more like a barrack. But because Tatay is the afternoon-shift foreman, we have a nicer, bigger place than most. There's a playground, baseball field, and tennis court for us to use, though I've only ever seen people play basketball on the tennis court. Never tennis.

It isn't so bad. Not all growers treat their workers as nicely as our boss does. Look at me, saying "our boss" like I work next to Tatay and

Nanay! I do help out, but only on weekends and days off from school. We have it pretty good where we live. I've heard stories of family housing on some ranches that's like metal boxes with no heat or running water. We're lucky. In our family housing, we have a newer, clean place to live with air conditioning and heat. Jasmine's house in town doesn't have air conditioning. Maybe that's why she spends so much time at my house, especially during summer.

The weather is warm in Delano and the soil is rich. Tatay says it's the best place he's ever seen for growing grapes. Whenever he says that, Nanay reminds him that France has all those famous vineyards too. She's kind of right. France's vineyards are so famous you don't think of Delano when someone says "grapes" or "wine," you think of France. At least I do, and I live here. Nanay talks about France like it's something special and how great life must be there all the way across the ocean. But I don't know why Nanay wants to go all the way to France to pick grapes when she can pick them right here.

There's two kinds of people in Delano. Growers, who own the ranches, and us—the workers that pick grapes. I say "us" and really mean it this time. Tatay works the field in the morning and then is a foreman of the afternoon crew. Lola says that's a really big "privilege." I think that just means the boss trusts him to do both jobs. Nanay works all day in the vineyard too. She doesn't pick grapes like Tatay. She packs them up and makes sure the size and quality are just right. If not, she sends the grapes to the winery. Lola used to be a packer when she was younger, but now she ties up grape vines with me. Isko says that's kids work, but I think work is work no matter what—especially when you get three cents a vine. It's fun to work alongside Lola, singing songs and having vine-girdling races. I can tie up a grapevine faster than anyone, even Isko. Jasmine says that's nothing to brag about, but I say if I can beat Isko at anything, I'm going to brag about it. Beating Isko at vine-girdling races and getting paid to do it? What's not to like?

Another thing I like, besides working with Lola and being better than Isko at something, is singing. When my family works, or really just anytime, we sing. Working. At home. You name it, there's a song mixed in. Singing makes the workday go faster and a little more fun, so I sing.

Jasmine doesn't sing nearly as much as I do. I asked her one time why she doesn't sing when we girdle vines and she said maybe it's because she's both Filipino and Mexican. She thinks maybe the song-for-every-occasion gene is passed down on her Filipino side instead of her Mexican side. Lola says Jasmine's Filipino and Mexican heritage is like being caught between two different worlds. But I think Jasmine is lucky that she has two heritages instead of one like me.

It's a good thing I'm writing all this down instead of talking! It will probably help me with my writing skills.

Adyos!
Tala

Chapter Two

September 2, 1965

Dear Diary,

When Jasmine dares me to do something, I always
do it. It's a game we started when we were five years
old, right before Jasmine's family moved to their house
in town. We knew we weren't going to see each other
every day so Jasmine dared me to make sure we played
together once a week. Once a week turned into three
days a week after school and every weekend. I see her
so often now that I can't imagine not seeing her for a
whole week!

Jasmine never dares me to do anything
reckless or something that can get me or anyone
else hurt. I'm reckless enough on my own that
I don't need Jasmine to dare me into that.
Jasmine's dares are more like a push, or in some
cases a shove, to move me out of my day dreams
and into real life. Who I am inside is sometimes
not who I show on the outside. Jasmine wants

the world to see the person she sees. So she pushes me.

Here's a short list of some of the things Jasmine has dared me to do:

• Try out for church choir because I'm a "million times better than Rosie." Rosie still got the solo because her mom is choir director, but I stand in front real proud and sing like no one is watching. Lola says that's the only way to make sure you put your heart and soul into your music.

• Write down my stories because "they're better than anything you see in the movies." Jasmine admits she's not the best judge on this dare because she only goes to the movies as a special treat, usually her birthday or holidays, but it still makes me feel good to know someone, somewhere likes my stories. My brain is so full of stories that it's hard for me to remember that someone might love them someday as much as Jasmine loves them now. That's why she dared me to write them down. The more I write down now, the more I'll have to share later.

• Write in this diary every day "so we can look back on it when we're grown." I don't think Jasmine or I will care about what we're thinking right now five, ten, or even fifty years from now, but I'll try to write as much as I can. Weekends are busy with girdling grapes and helping with packing, but I'll try.

The thing is, nothing exciting happens in Delano. There isn't anything worth writing about unless you're really interested in grapes and farming. Jasmine says even ordinary things are extraordinary depending on how you look at them. She says a sunset can look like a beautiful art show the sky is painting instead of just meaning the day is over. And she calls me the artistic one! Jasmine has a better imagination than she thinks. She's practical, but always thinks things around here will be different someday, no matter how much she wants them to stay the same.

I want to experience new and different things too, but I know I'm not going to find them around here. I won't even find them in Bakersfield. Someday, I'm going to have to go far away to find excitement. It makes me a little sad, though. I don't want to grow up and leave Tatay, Nanay, Lola, and Jasmine, but I can't stop dreaming either.

Jasmine understands this . . . sort of. She flip-flops between following her dreams and staying put. I know we don't have to decide *anything yet, but I wish we could just pick a path for my future now. I think life throws distractions and what-ifs at me to make me doubt my dreams. But I still see my dreams so clearly it feels like I can reach out and touch them.*

I'm going to keep reaching.

Tala

Tala and Jasmine climbed to the top of the play structure outside of the ranch family housing. The girls watched the sun set over the vineyard, turning everything the light touched orange and purple. The play structure was a new addition at the family housing complex, as was the tennis court and baseball field. Tala was excited when she first heard the grower was building all those play and sport options at the ranch. Tatay was angry. He paced around the kitchen, muttering how a new playground wasn't going to make up for the poor working conditions and low pay they gave their workers.

"Where are you going to be in ten years?" Jasmine asked suddenly, looking at the setting sun instead of at Tala.

"What do you mean?" Tala threw a rock off the top of the play structure, listening to it thump on the ground.

"I mean what I said." Jasmine bit her lower lip and shrugged. "'Cause all I see for me is grapes, grapes, and more grapes. Even if I leave this vineyard, I don't see me

escaping it. It follows you, you know? If you were born into it, there's no way out. At least that's what it feels like."

"There's more out there for you than just grapes." Tala was sure her best friend was meant for great things, even if Jasmine didn't know it yet herself.

"What if we're just stuck here?" she asked. "What if this sunset is all we're ever going to see of the world, Tala?"

"Don't say that," Tala shook her head. "That's giving up. You want to see the world? See it. Don't let Delano be the only thing you see. Imagine yourself somewhere special—imagine yourself *as* someone special—and it will happen."

"This isn't like making a wish on birthday candles, Tala." Jasmine sounded bitter. "This is real life. *Our* life." She shook her head. "I know you dream big enough for the both of us. But I can't see past my feet on the ground."

"Just because a wish might not come true doesn't mean you should stop making wishes," Tala insisted. "Yeah, wishes don't always come true, but I don't ever want to be so practical and so feet-on-the-ground that I forget how to wish."

"So 'feet-on-the-ground'?" Jasmine repeated. "Kind of like me?"

"That's not what I meant."

Both girls were silent as they watched the sun sink low in the sky.

"Where do I think I'll be in ten years?" Tala repeated Jasmine's question. "That's easy. I'm going to be a newspaper writer. Who knows? Maybe I'll work for *El Malcriado* one day."

"Chávez's paper? The Voice of the Farmworker?" Jasmine asked.

"Yes. I could tell other people's stories every week."

Jasmine smiled. "What about me, Tala?" she asked. "When you're off reporting stories, what am I going to do? What are your dreams for me?"

"In ten years, you'll be living far away from here in New York City." Tala had a dreamy look on her face. "You'll have your own little restaurant to teach those New Yorkers what real Filipino food tastes like."

Jasmine laughed. "New Yorkers wouldn't know kare-kare from beef stew."

"That's why they need you to teach them." Tala nudged Jasmine's shoulder with hers. "They need you to save them from themselves and their uninspired food choices. Chef Jasmine to the rescue."

Jasmine slung her arm around Tala's shoulders as the sun finally disappeared completely from view. "Let's try to write in our diaries every day. That way we can always remember times like this when it was just us, the sun, and our dreams."

Tala smiled. "Us, the sun, and our dreams. I like the sound of that. Let's do it."

Jasmine held out her crooked pinkie finger. "Pinkie swear?"

Tala linked her finger with Jasmine's. "Pinkie swear."

Chapter Three

September 5, 1965
Dear Diary,

Nanay and Tatay are hiding something. I just know it! I don't mean something like a birthday present they hid in the coat closet and then forgot all about it till now. I mean they're hiding something more mysterious. A real secret. The kind of secret you stop talking about when other people (like me) come into the room.

They do that sometimes, stop talking when I enter a room. Our apartment isn't that big, and sometimes there's important AWOC business to discuss that they don't want me to know about. AWOC stands for Agricultural Workers Organizing Committee, so "important AWOC business" is usually something about work conditions and safety. I know they've talked to *the growers before about better pay, better access to toilets and water, and setting up rules like not working in the fields if it's over 100 degrees, but somehow it feels different this time. More urgent.*

I know Nanay and Tatay won't tell me anything, so I think I'm going to start with Lola. What does she know? I'm going to help her with dinner tonight so hopefully I will find something out!

Till I have more to report . . .

Adyos!
Tala

"Lola?" Tala asked. "Why do Nanay and Tatay stop talking when I come in a room? It's happened a bunch of times in the last few weeks. Is something going on?"

Lola hummed while frying a batch of lumpia in the wok, seemingly oblivious to Tala's question.

Tala narrowed her eyes. *Is she ignoring me? This must mean she really does know something.*

"Why do Nanay and Tatay leave when I come in?" Tala pressed.

"You're imagining things, Nene. You see shadows that aren't there." Lola spooned the pork lumpia filling into a wrapper and rolled it into a cylinder shape as she talked. Then she pinched the ends shut, sealing the filling inside. "Your parents are just busy with work, that's all."

"No, it seems like more than that," Tala insisted. "If they were busy with work, they'd just be tired, not whispering in corners and leaving rooms when I come in. Something is going on. Why won't anyone tell me what?"

"What do you hear? Or think you hear?" Lola added quickly.

Tala shrugged. "That's the thing, I can't hear anything if they don't talk in front of me. At first, I thought it was about my birthday, but my birthday was almost a week ago and the whispering hasn't stopped."

"There's always something to whisper about." Lola winked at Tala. "Some words just hold more weight than others."

Tala threw her head back and groaned. *Is this how a real investigative reporter feels when their source isn't cooperating? It is so frustrating!* "You're not going to help me, are you?"

Lola tended to the lumpia. "Sometimes, Nene, we need to help ourselves."

Chapter Four

"Hay naku!" Tala exclaimed. "When my parents want to keep a secret, they really keep a secret!"

Tala and Jasmine were in their side-by-side desks at school. Tala ran her hands over her long, black braids, lost in thought.

"You haven't figured it out yet, huh?" Jasmine responded.

Tala shook her head. "My first three days as an investigative reporter were a bust. All I found out is that everyone is acting strange—even Lola. It's like they all got together and decided to keep a giant secret from me. And I can't find any clues because no one is giving me a straight answer."

"Maybe them being weird *is* the clue you need to follow to kick your investigation into high gear," Jasmine suggested.

"What do you mean?" Tala asked.

"If everyone is acting weird, it means everyone has the same secret," Jasmine said. "You just need to figure out what that is."

"I just need to figure out what it is," Tala repeated before grinning. "That's it! Jasmine, you're amazing!"

Jasmine blushed at her best friend's praise. "I'm not amazing. I'm just being practical."

"Well, practical is amazing," Tala said. "I know what I need to do to look for answers. Meet me out front after school. I want you to come with me."

After the school dismissal bell rang, Jasmine, Isko, and Tala walked to the grocery store where the vineyard land meets the road to Delano.

Ding.

Mr. Montoya looked up from behind the grocery-store counter when the bell above the door rang to signal customers.

"Good afternoon," he said, greeting his newest visitors with a warm smile. "Are you here for some candy?"

Mr. and Mrs. Montoya, the family that ran the grocery store, always gave out one free penny candy from the candy jars. It was a sales trick to make customers buy more after the free sample, but Tala usually stopped at just one candy. While her family was not bankrupt, Tala did not did not have extra spending money each month, but free was something she could always afford.

"She'll take a peppermint," Jasmine pointed at Tala.

"And she'll take a lemon drop," Tala pointed at Jasmine, giggling at their predicable choices.

"Don't forget about me!" Isko screeched right next to Tala's ear.

He's so annoying, Tala thought.

"I'll take a lemon drop too," Isko continued, then gave Tala a winning smile.

"One a penny, two a penny, three a penny, four." Mr. Montoya counted out three penny candies and slid the fourth across the counter to his son Alex. Alex was Isko's friend, but Tala didn't think he was as annoying as Isko was. *Except*, Tala thought, *anyone would be considered "not as annoying" when compared to Isko.*

Tala chewed and swallowed the last bit of peppermint in her mouth. It was time. Tala turned to Mr. Montoya. "I'm doing some research for . . . a story I'm writing. A news story. Have you seen anyone acting funny over the last couple days? Anyone at all?"

Mr. Montoya thought a moment. Tala could practically see him rewinding the days in his head to find anything that seemed out of the ordinary. "There's something that stuck out to me a day or so ago. Larry Itliong asked if I ever take store credit for goods instead of cash."

"Why was that so unusual?" Tala asked.

"Well, I told him I accept credit—we always have and always will—but it also depends on the circumstances and who is doing the asking."

"What do you mean?" Tala asked.

Mr. Montoya chuckled. "You certainly have a lot of questions! I understand most farmworkers are cash poor and pay depends on a lot of circumstances that can be out of their control. I know that if I were in their shoes, I'd want to be able to buy necessities even if the crop wasn't yielding as expected or if I got sick. Seems a shame that when your productivity goes down, so does your pay."

"So what did Itliong say to that?"

"Nothing. He just thanked me and left. Didn't even buy anything."

"Yeah, but a lot of people leave the store without buying something," Alex pointed out.

Mr. Montoya nodded slowly. "They do, but this was different. It was like he was planning for something."

Something's coming, Tala thought to herself. *I don't know what yet, but it's a start.*

Then Tala said, "Thanks, Mr. Montoya. And thanks for the candy."

She hurried out of the store with Jasmine and Isko close behind her. A plan was starting to take shape in Tala's head as they walked back to her house.

"Everyone—not just my parents—is hiding something, and we're going to figure out what it is," Tala said as they walked. "I'm still not quite sure what that something is, but I think I might know what's going on. Or at least I will in a couple of days if my guess is right."

"Leave me out of it," Isko said. "I'm not getting in trouble because you came up with some crazy plan in that crazy brain of yours."

"Tala isn't crazy." Jasmine pinched her brother's arm in her best friend's defense. He yelped an "ow" before glaring at both of the girls. "Mama and Papa *have* been acting funny, Isko. They're quiet and . . . um, what's the word you like to use, Tala, when someone isn't being bright and flashy like they normally are?"

"Subdued?" Tala offered.

Jasmine nodded. "Yeah, Isko, what Tala said. Mama and Papa have been quiet and subdued. Something's not right. I feel it too. Maybe the grapes are being eaten by bugs or the owners are letting workers go. I don't know. If Mama and Papa are hiding stuff from us, I want to know what it is."

"And how exactly are you going to do that?" Isko crossed his arms over his chest. "All your plans will go up in smoke if Mama and Papa know you're catching on to them. Yeah, they're keeping secrets, but you gotta keep 'em right back, Jaz."

Isko giving advice is about as common as snow is in California, Tala thought. *Maybe he knows more than he's letting on.*

Tala eyed Isko suspiciously. "Why are you helping us?" she asked him. "You just said you didn't want anything to do with it."

"I don't want anything to do with your dumb plan," Isko agreed. "But I also don't want you chasing false stories, Tala. If you think something is going on with the workers, go to an AWOC meeting."

As soon as Isko mentioned the workers' organization committee meeting, it was like a light bulb went off in Tala's head.

"That's it!" Tala grabbed Jasmine's arm and looked her straight in the eyes. "We need to listen in on the next AWOC meeting." She grinned as the excitement of chasing a story took over. "This could be the big break in my case, Jaz. There's a story out there, and I'm going to tell it."

Chapter Five

September 7, 1965
Dear Diary,

I have a plan that I hope will get me some answers. It's going to take a lot of things going right, but if they do, this could be the break I need!

Jasmine thinks the plan is too complicated, but I've convinced her that we at least need to try. How am I ever going to be an investigative reporter if I don't take risks to investigate anything?

I have to go now but I'll write when I can!

Tala

"We're happy you were able to stay for dinner, Jasmine, but it's getting late." Nanay's voice was distant and distracted as she wiped the kitchen counter down with a dishrag even though it was already spotless. She kept looking at the clock and then out the window as if expecting something.

"But Jasmine can't go home!" Tala screeched. "We have a group project we're working on. It's due tomorrow."

"You should have thought of that before you waited until the last minute to finish it," Tatay said as he entered the kitchen. He fidgeted with his watch before doing the same look-at-the-clock, look-out-the-window motion as Nanay.

"It's not last minute," Tala said. "It's under pressure. I do my best work under pressure."

Tatay laughed before tugging on one of her braids. "It's called procrastination, Tala, but nice try."

"My parents wouldn't mind if I stay over," Jasmine jumped in. "I can call them to make sure."

Jasmine got up to call her mom. After a short exchange, she handed the phone to Nanay. "Mama wants to double-check with you that it's okay if I sleep over."

Tala gave Jasmine thumbs up sign. The plan was working! It was really working!

After Jasmine handed the phone off to Nanay, Tala motioned for Jasmine to follow her to the bedroom she shared with Lola.

Once they were safe in Tala's bedroom, Jasmine collapsed onto the bed "Whew! I was so scared Mama would tell me to just come home. She'd ruin everything!"

"Now I just hope they don't find out there is no group project we're supposed to be working on," Tala said.

Jasmine crossed her fingers on both hands. "Do you think we'll really find out why everyone's been so secretive tonight?"

"We have to try."

Tatay and Nanay came into Tala's bedroom ten minutes later to check on the girls. They found them hard at work on their project.

"We might be late tonight," Nanay warned. "Can I trust you girls to put yourselves to bed? No staying up to gossip. It's a school night."

"Of course, Nanay." Tala smiled as big as possible. "I know you have the AWOC meeting tonight, but didn't you just have one yesterday? Why so many meetings lately?"

"We're just discussing something that didn't go over so well last night," Tatay said. "The members went home and slept on it and changed their minds, that's all."

"Changed their minds about what?" Tala asked.

Tatay leaned down to kiss Tala on the forehead before tugging her braid. "Unfortunately, I can't tell you anything about that right now. If all goes as planned tonight, I'll be able to tell you more tomorrow."

"Do you promise?" Tala asked.

Tatay nodded and pulled on her braid one last time. "I promise. Good night, girls."

"Good night!" Jasmine and Tala chorused.

The girls stared at each other for a few moments until they heard the door slam behind Tala's parents.

"Wow, there really is something going on!" Jasmine whispered excitedly. "How long do we wait to follow them?"

"As soon as I check on Lola." Lola and Tala shared a room, but Lola never went to bed before her favorite shows were over. Lola had saved up for almost a whole year for a small TV set. She made sure to get her money's worth out of it. Tala hoped they could sneak out to the AWOC meeting and get home before Lola even came to bed.

Tala crept out of her room and peeked around the corner into the living room. *Bonanza* was on, and Lola was engrossed. *The only thing she'd notice is if the electricity went out and interrupted her show*, Tala thought.

Tala hurried back to Jasmine. "Let's go!"

The girls climbed out the window and followed the dirt road to the AWOC headquarters at Filipino Hall.

As they walked up the path to the hall, they could hear chattering voices.

"How are we going to get inside? Won't they see us?" Jasmine looked worried.

Tala hadn't thought that far ahead. She looked around.

"There," she pointed to a discarded grape crate. "Let's stand on that and watch from the window."

The girls moved the crate under a side window, climbed on top, and peeked inside.

Larry Itliong called the meeting to order. He was a short man with thick glasses, an army-style buzz cut, and three fingers missing on his right hand. When he spoke, the crowd immediately hushed to hear what he had to say.

"Well?" he asked, surveying the crowd. "Yesterday, you came to me saying you wanted to strike. You wanted to be like the workers in Coachella and Bakersfield. You wanted to bring their fight to Delano. I told you what you'd face if we voted to strike. I told you if we vote yes you'll be in danger of losing your car, losing your job, and going hungry. Voting to strike is not something to take lightly." He stopped to take a drink of water.

"If we strike, the growers will try to crush us. They'll try to put us down and make sure our demands never get past words on a paper. Voting yes to strike sets us up for a fight, but the growers will fight right back. Is that what you

want?" Tala shivered as his words reverberated through the packed hall.

He continued, "Yesterday, the answer was no. Only one person raised their hand when I asked who was ready to vote for the strike. Now you say you've changed your minds. What changed?"

A man in the front stood up. "We needed time to think, and now we have."

Tala gasped. It was Tatay!

"Growers don't take our requests seriously. They think if they don't show up to meetings with AWOC representatives we will just quietly go away or resign ourselves to our lot in life. We need to show them we cannot be ignored. We need to vote to strike."

Then Tatay turned to the crowd. "The Filipino workers in Coachella voted to strike in May and now make one dollar and forty cents an hour plus twenty-five cents per box of grapes picked. That agreement wasn't honored when they came up to help in Delano."

"Growers pay us just one dollar and twenty-five cents an hour and ten cents per box," another man added.

"We're just asking for a contract that will treat everyone with dignity and justice." Tatay spread his arms out wide. "If striking is the way to achieve our goals, then we strike."

Itliong stood silently in front of the delegation. He brought his right hand up to his chin as if considering Tatay's words. "If we put it to a vote, you can't come back tomorrow and say you changed your mind again. If we strike, we follow it through till we're heard."

The delegation started to talk all at once.

After calling the meeting back to order, Itliong put it to a vote. Each member came up one by one to cast a paper ballot in a locked box.

"So it is settled," Itliong said after tallying the results. "We strike!"

"What does that mean?" Jasmine asked. Tala could barely hear her over the shouts inside the hall.

"It means no one goes to work until the growers treat everyone fairly," Tala said. The reality of the strike hit Tala like a train. *If Tatay doesn't work, how will he earn money? And how are we supposed to live without money?*

Chapter Six

Tatay did not go to work the next day. When Tala woke up and got ready for school, he was just sitting calmly at the kitchen table reading a newspaper.

"Tatay?" Tala wasn't sure what to say without letting on that she knew about the strike. "Aren't you going to work today?"

"I'm taking an . . . unscheduled vacation, Nene," he said.

Tala chewed on her bottom lip. She knew some people took vacations for fun, but her family never had enough time or money for one.

"For how long?" she asked.

"For as long as it takes to make sure everyone who works at the ranch is treated fairly." He took a sip of his coffee.

Tala opened and closed her mouth like a fish out of water.

Knock knock.

There was someone at the door. Nanay went to see who it was.

"Danilo," Nanay said to Tatay. "The foreman is here."

Tatay nodded and stood up to meet his visitor. When he stepped outside, Tala ran to the window. Nanay came up beside her and cracked the window open just a bit so they could make out the men's words.

"Michael." Tatay nodded to the foreman. He kept his voice pleasant, like there was nothing wrong with skipping work. "What can I do for you this morning?"

"I'm just going around checking on why none of my crew showed up to work this morning," the foreman said. "Care to enlighten me on why that's happening?"

"The AWOC sent over our list of demands," Tatay said. "We've been trying to negotiate with the growers for months. All they do in return is stonewall us. Tell the boss to read our demands. When they are ready to negotiate, so are we."

"'Demands' is a strong word, there, Danilo." The foreman crossed his arms over his chest. "The AWOC should know you catch more flies with honey than with vinegar."

"Sorry, Michael, we're all out of honey."

By the time Tatay returned to the kitchen, Nanay and Tala were sitting at the table. Tala had a ton of questions but wasn't sure if asking them would make Tatay angry or upset.

Jasmine wandered in from the bathroom, rubbing sleep from her eyes, still tired from the girls' late night. "What's going on?" She looked down the line of concerned faces standing around the living room. "Is everything okay?"

"Tatay?" Tala's voice was a mix of confusion and hope.

"Finish getting ready for school, Nene," he said. "I'll walk with you and Jasmine."

Chapter Seven

September 9, 1965
Dear Diary,

It seems funny that just one week ago, I wrote that nothing happens in Delano. One week seems like a lifetime ago now.

Tatay called a family meeting tonight. He talked about the strike.

"By now, I'm sure you know things are a little different with work," Tatay began. "I want you to prepare for what's ahead. This is not going to be easy, but nothing worth doing ever is. The AWOC has a chance to really bring about change. We're not just talking about it, we're finally doing something. I can't even say how proud that makes me."

Proud. Tatay is proud of what the AWOC is trying to do. Proud has always been one of those strange words to me that people say but don't really mean. They say they're proud of their job, but do they really mean it? When Tatay says he's proud of my good work in school, I can tell he means it. His eyes sparkle, he smiles, and his chest puffs out a little bit. He's never been "proud" of field work. He works hard, but when he mentions the strike, I can tell he really IS proud and not just pretending.

"We're the voice that will shine a bright light on our community," Tatay said. "That doesn't come without a price, though. We might get pushed around or picked on. People we usually consider our friends might turn their backs on us. Our food budget will be tight. We might need to go to the church for charity or hope for donations from supporters once word of the strike spreads. We have some money set aside, but it's not going to stretch forever. Starting now, we need to take stock of what we can and can't live without. I know I'm asking a lot of you. There are so many things that could go wrong with this strike. But there are also so many things that could go right. The most important thing is we need to show the growers a united front, no matter what. Everyone involved in the strike is our family in the field and we need to treat them like family."

"Is the strike just about more money?" I asked.

Tatay shook his head. "No, Nene, I wish it were that simple. Negotiating higher wages is an important reason behind the strike, but we can't, and won't, stop at that. There's so much more work to be done."

Then Tatay told horror stories about the working conditions at some of the other ranches. We were fortunate to have what most considered a "good boss." But even a good boss didn't provide access to some necessities like water and easy-to-access portable toilets. Without toilets, many workers relieved themselves in the fields . . . the same fields they had to work in all day.

Other field workers were sprayed with the chemicals meant to treat the grapes, didn't get overtime pay, or worked ten-plus hours in the heat for little more than twelve dollars a day. If you got sick, you got sick. There was always someone else to take your spot in the fields and your pay if you couldn't work.

Some growers charged twenty-five cents for a cup of water. And the cup wasn't even a cup but a used soda can and shared by everyone who bought water! Tatay does his best to shield me from the worst of the working conditions, but he can't shield me from the stories. How could anyone treat another human being in such a cruel, careless manner? Grape workers aren't animals. Even animals deserve better. Hay naku!

I wish there was more I could do to help the strike. I want to be a part of the action. I know by supporting Tatay and Nanay I support the strike, but it feels like something is still missing. I know I'm young and can't strike like Tatay, but there's got to be other ways I can show my support.

Tala

Chapter Eight

"You said a day, Danilo, maybe three, but it's been a week and the growers aren't even talking to the AWOC," Nanay said. "It's a joke to them. You're a joke to them."

"That's not true." Tatay followed Nanay around the living room. Tala watched them both from her spot at the kitchen table. Nanay never stayed still when upset.

"We just need more time," Tatay continued. "We're not a joke to the growers. They're just trying to wait us out. The strikers in Coachella saw this tactic too. The growers start with silence, and then when that doesn't send us back to the fields, they bring in non-union scab labor. They want us to break the strike. If we don't, then they negotiate."

"Negotiate?" Nanay whirled around to face Tatay. "More time? You're wasting what little savings we have while you give the growers more time! Not everyone can sit around and wait, Danilo. You voted to do something, and

I said I would support you, but now you do nothing." She threw her hands up in exasperation.

Tatay moved to put his arm around Nanay. "Itliong has plans," he said. "We're bringing in the NFWA. They're young, but they've been very successful across in the region with just this sort of situation. By working together—"

"The National Farm Workers Association?" Nanay interrupted, shrugging his arm off her shoulders. "Chávez's group? If the Mexicans wanted to join us, they would have done it already."

"They're our brothers in the fields, why not be our brothers in the strike?" Tatay forked both hands through his dark hair in agitation.

"The truth is, we caught them off guard," Tatay continued. "The NFWA have been planning a strike for the exact same reasons we went in for. They just wanted to be able to fund it, so they waited. If we bring them in, we'll be able to combine their funds with AWOC's to pay striking workers and anything else we need. Itliong has decades of experience with strikes. If this is what he wants to do, I trust him. By uniting the groups, we're ensuring the growers can't use the Mexicans against the Filipinos and vice versa to break the strike."

Nanay sighed in agitation. "I know you think you're doing the admirable thing, Danilo, but did you think about how it would affect everyone?" She motioned to Tala. "We're all sick of eating beans and rice and it's only been a week! What if this goes on longer? And we're lucky to have food! What about the families that didn't prepare like we did? It'll ruin them, and all because you think you're doing what is right."

"It *is* right," Tatay insisted. "Change isn't possible if you just stand still."

Nanay rolled her eyes. "Yes, but you can't do anything if you don't have money for food to eat." She stormed off to their bedroom, slamming the door behind her.

Tatay and Tala looked at each other, the silence echoing louder than any words or actions ever could.

"It will be all right, Nene," he assured Tala. "Everything is going to be all right."

"Tala!" Jasmine shrieked and ran to hug Tala at school the next day. "Papa and Mama say we might have to move! I don't want to move. I don't know anywhere else but Delano."

"Move?" Tala felt like time slowed down to a crawl. Everything from her thoughts to her words oozed out as slow as molasses when hit with Jasmine's news. "Why?"

"Papa says we can't live where there's no work," she said. "If they can't work, they can't pay rent or buy food. It's not just Papa and Mama, but my older brothers too. Everyone is out of work from the strike. If we break the strike and go back to work, we stay. If not, we go."

"But don't you believe in what the workers are fighting for?" Tala asked.

"Of course we do," Jasmine said. "But Papa says belief doesn't put money in your pockets and food on the table."

Tala hugged Jasmine tight. "I don't want you to go!"

"I don't want to go either, but my parents say we can't last the week unless we break the strike."

Tala hugged her best friend even tighter. She used to think the strike was like a big adventure. If the Perez family moved away because of it, it would quickly turn into a nightmare.

Chapter Nine

The Perez family couldn't afford to strike. With a large family and a small savings account, it wasn't long before Mr. Perez rejoined the field workers and Mrs. Perez took up her formerly empty place in the packing house.

Word spread quickly through town that the Perez family broke the strike. Jasmine saw an immediate backlash at school.

"Scab," someone whispered as Tala and Jasmine searched for a cafeteria table at lunchtime. Tala flinched. She knew the taunts were directed at Jasmine, but she felt like she was being accused too.

It seemed like the words were coming from all directions. *Scab . . . Scab . . . We don't want your kind here . . . No scabs allowed.*

Tala watched as Jasmine frantically looked around the lunch room, trying to find the source of the taunts.

"Your family would have done the same thing if it would help you to survive," she challenged the unknown accusers. "We just want to be left alone."

A tall boy in Isko's grade stood up to face Jasmine. "You should have thought of that before you broke the strike." He took a step closer and leaned in. "Now you're just a scab. And what do we do with scabs? We pick at them until they're gone."

The bully heaped a spoonful of mashed potatoes onto his fork and flung it at Jasmine. Tala gasped. The potatoes landed right between Jasmine's eyes and oozed down her nose, mouth, and chin before sliding onto her white shirt. Jasmine looked over at Tala for help but Tala stood there frozen and silent.

This can't be happening, Tala thought. It was as if the scene were happening to someone else instead of her best friend.

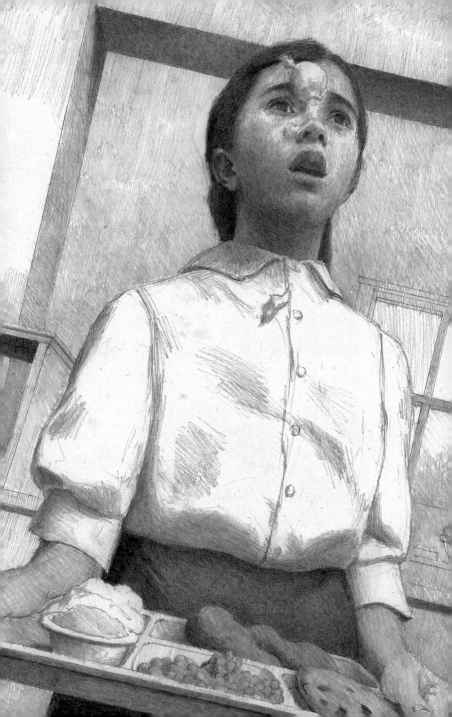

A sob broke free before Jasmine could stop it. No one stopped her from running away.

Tala found Jasmine crying in the bathroom ten minutes later.

"Jasmine?" she said hesitantly. "I looked all over for you. Are you all right?"

"Why didn't you say something?" Jasmine growled. "Why didn't you *do* something, Tala? When I needed you most, you acted like I was a complete stranger."

"That's not true." Tala said defensively. "I—I didn't know what to say."

"You always know what to say," Jasmine spat.

Tala took a deep breath. *This is your best friend*, she thought. *Now is the time to come together, not break apart.* She took her friend's hand and guided her out of the stall. The girls sat on the radiator on the wall.

"I don't always know what to say," Tala said. "I didn't know what to say to make that bully stop. I wish I did. I wish I could rewind and start all over again. I promise to stand up the next time you need me, Jasmine." Tala held out her crooked pinkie finger. "Pinkie swear."

Jasmine smiled through her tears and reached out with her own finger. "Pinkie swear."

SCABS ARE PEOPLE TOO

By Tala Mendoza

It is easy to get caught up in "strike mania." What side are you on? Do you support the little guys (the workers) or the big guys (the growers)? It's like a modern-day David and Goliath. While David threw rocks to target Goliath's weakness, the workers haven't found the growers' weakness yet. Growers seem content to sit back in their fancy houses and wait for the Davids of the strike to give up the fight and come back to work. Goliath thought he was invincible, and maybe the growers feel the same way. Everything has been one way—their way—for generations. They don't know what to do when the little guys try to change the rules. Which side are you on? Who is right and who is wrong?

Nothing is just black or white, only shades of gray.

The demands of the strikers are important. Workers need to be paid a living wage. Working conditions need to be improved. But striking comes at a cost. Some workers, especially those with families, can't afford to go on strike. These people are bullied daily because their families chose putting food on the table over the strike. They believe in everything the AWOC and NFWA are doing, they just can't support it with the loss of their job.

Think about this the next time you see someone cross the picket line. Everyone has a story. What is theirs?

September 17, 1965
Dear Diary,

I am so excited! I finally found a way I can help the strike. I'm going to use all these words that are bumping around in my head.

There's a mimeograph machine at Filipino Hall I can use to make copies of my articles. I'll pass them out at church, school, the grocery store . . . wherever I can. Tatay even said he could take some with him to the picket line.

Now I can practice being a journalist and do more than just observing in the background.

Tala

"I heard the bosses are bringing in scab laborers," someone said. "Out with the old, in with the new. If you're not thankful to have a job, you should lose it."

It was Sunday. Church day. Tala was distributing her news article. Tatay, Nanay, and Lola sat in their usual pew. The Mendozas were there early because even though Lola didn't like to admit it, she loved gossiping with the other grandmothers before the service.

"I bet even the scabs won't want to work for a dollar twenty an hour," Lola said. "A job is important, yes, but so is being able to support your family."

"No one is supporting anyone when they stay home instead of going to the fields," someone else said.

"Who needs out-of-state scabs when we got scabs right here?"

Tala stopped distributing her fliers to turn and see who the woman was pointing at. The Perez family stood in the doorway, the light from the outside shining on them like a spotlight. Tala and Jasmine's eyes met. Jasmine's hand shook as she lifted it to brush her brown hair away from her face. She tried to smile, but it disappeared from her lips almost as soon as it appeared.

"Scab," one of the parishioners hissed. "How dare you show your face in church? Go away. We don't want you here."

Usually, Jasmine and her family sat by the Mendozas, but when they tried to make their way to the pew, people blocked them. Arms. Legs. Purses. Anything to keep the Perezes from descending the aisle of the church.

"We don't want you here, scab," someone growled. "You picked your side. Stay on it."

Tala couldn't believe her eyes. She took in the scene of her church: on one side of the aisle sat strike supporters, the other side sat families that had broken the strike. *But church is supposed to be a place where we come together.*

Tala saw Jasmine's mama's lower lip tremble, but Mrs. Perez held her head high as she ushered her large family over to the "scab side" of the aisle.

Tala tried to concentrate on the service but found it difficult to do so. She heard whispers of "scab" in the open spaces and saw people ball up and toss her news article at the Perez family and other strikebreakers.

Mrs. Perez may have been too proud to cry in front of the congregation, but Jasmine wasn't. By the end of the service, she was openly crying. Tala couldn't sit still and watch her best friend be hurt. She didn't come to her rescue at school, but she would now.

As the final hymn was sung, Tala jumped to her feet. "What is wrong with you people?" she shrieked. Nanay desperately grabbed at her arm to get her to sit back down, but Tala shook free of her mother's hands and ran down the aisle to the pulpit.

Tala stood at the front of the congregation. The choir had stopped singing and all eyes were on her.

"What happened to 'Do unto others as you would have them do unto you'? Is this how you want to be treated? Name calling and throwing trash? I thought you were grownups. Well, act like it. Just because the Perezes and other families need to work, doesn't mean they don't support the strike. All it means is they need money and food."

Tatay stood and joined Tala at the pulpit. "There are other ways to support the strike. Pass out AWOC pamphlets. Cook a meal for a striking friend. This is the time for us to be united, not to fall apart. Let's not forget we are trying to create a better future for ourselves and our children."

Tala hugged Tatay around the waist. "Thank you," she whispered.

Chapter Ten

September 19, 1965
Dear Diary,

Sometimes I think Tatay understands me more than Nanay. I love Nanay, but Tatay believes in the same things I do. He believes that if we shine a light on everything bad in life, good will come out of it. I want to believe that no matter how many times ugliness shows itself, hope is stronger than fear. It's easy to be afraid. It's easy to stand back and watch the bad happen around you instead of standing up and doing something. It's hard to hope. It's hard to imagine that things could be better in the future if we change them today.

Tatay is going to another vote at Filipino Hall tomorrow. The NFWA will be there; they're voting on whether they will join our strike or not. I asked Tatay if I could come with so I can write a story about it, but he said no. He didn't even ask Nanay if she wanted to go to the meeting. Even I know her answer would be "no." The longer the strike goes on, the more upset Nanay becomes. Maybe things will be over more quickly if the NFWA votes to strike too.

Will Mexicans and Filipinos join together? I'll know after the vote!

Tala

September 20, 1965
Dear Diary,

The NFWA joined the strike today. Papa says that means everyone will be back to work soon and we won't be called scabs anymore. I hope he's right. I don't tell Mama and Papa half the stuff that goes on at school since the strike started. Isko gets caught fighting almost every day but won't tell them why. I promised not to say anything. He's just trying to protect me and Amala (and himself) from the bullies. You can't always do with that words. Sometimes it takes fists.

    For the first time since the strike started, I'm hopeful it will be over soon. Together, the NFWA and AWOC should have more power to get results. Chávez takes a lot of his ideas from Gandhi and Dr. Martin Luther King Jr. He believes it's okay to protest, but it should be done peacefully. Strikers' pledge of nonviolence doesn't stop growers and their supporters from spraying protesters with pesticide, stomping on toes, and blowing up signs with shotguns. But nonviolence will hopefully get workers attention and sympathy from the people who matter—the people who buy grapes. By getting attention, the workers will get their demands met. Papa says the growers won't ignore the workers anymore now that the AWOC has united with the NFWA. For me, the two unions joining forces has a special meaning.

Being both Filipino and Mexican, I've always felt a little like I was on the outside looking in. I was pulled in two different directions. Now that the two groups are coming together, I feel complete. I never knew just how out of place I felt until I didn't have to worry about it anymore.

Jasmine

LARRY ITLIONG: THE SPARK THAT STARTED A MOVEMENT

By Tala Mendoza

News of César Chávez and the NFWA joining the grape strike may be dominating the news on everything from TV to newspapers, but there's one man who has been on the front line of workers' rights for over thirty years.

Manong Larry Itliong is no stranger to the picket line. He's been organizing and participating in strikes for more than half his life. From asparagus fields to Alaskan canneries, Itliong has fought for the rights of workers and won.

In May, Filipino workers in Coachella went on strike. They weren't able to negotiate a contract with growers, but were able to get a rate hike from $1.20 to $1.40 an hour. When those same workers followed the grape harvest to Delano, they found their agreement wasn't honored outside of Coachella. What good was a pay increase agreement with growers if it only worked in one town? The workers were the same, even if the location changed.

The workers took their concerns to Larry Itliong and the Delano chapter of AWOC in a special meeting at Filipino Hall. Could workers survive two strikes in four months? Could they stand the possibility of losing their cars, houses, and possessions if the strike lasted for a long time? At first, the workers voted "no" to the strike. But the next day, that "no" turned to "yes."

The Filipino AWOC and Mexican NFWA have not worked together before. In fact, their work in the past often undercut each other: if one went on strike, the other would take over the jobs of the striking workers, or "scab." This time it is different. Itliong called the two groups to work together. He asked Chávez for help, and now they've joined together. Workers are hopeful that the merging of these two unions will make them more effective than they are apart.

"*D*o you think your parents will come back to the strike now that the NFWA is involved?" Tala asked Jasmine. They were sitting on the swings on the school playground.

Tala didn't wait for an answer. "I hope so. It feels like I never see you anymore. I mean, I know we sit next to each other at school, but we don't hang out like we used to."

"I know. You're always welcome at my house though," Jasmine said. "Mama said so."

"And you're always welcome at my house," Tala said. "But then why do I only see you at school and church?"

Jasmine sighed. "Mama doesn't want us out on our own. You know . . . in case something happens."

Tala's eyebrows shot up. "Like what?"

Jasmine shot Tala a you-know-what look. "Mama just doesn't think it's safe, that's all."

"Has anything else happened that you haven't told me about?" Tala asked.

Jasmine shrugged. "Nothing you need to worry about."

Tala reached out to grab Jasmine's hand. She waited till her best friend looked up at her before squeezing her hand in a show of support. "I pinkie swore, remember?" she said quietly. "I'll stick up for you, no matter what."

Jasmine chewed on her bottom lip, thinking over Tala's words. "Words don't solve everything."

"They should." Tala let go of Jasmine's hand.

Both girls were silent for a long moment, lost in their own thoughts, before Tala asked her question again. "Do you think your parents will come back to the strike?"

Jasmine shook her head. "Papa says he still needs to earn a living, no matter who is running the show." Jasmine half-heartedly pumped her legs to make her swing move back and forth. "I'm glad both sides are agreeing that something should be done. I wish the same would happen at home. Mama wants one thing, Papa wants another. No one can agree on anything."

"Same here." Tala didn't feel like swinging, so she just dragged her feet in the gravel. "Tatay and Nanay always saw eye-to-eye until the strike vote. Now it's like she blames him for everything, even when it's not his fault. Lola stays out of it. I feel stuck in the middle."

"If you were older, what side would you be on?" Jasmine asked.

"Who needs to be older?" Tala laughed. "I know already. I'd vote for better working conditions and pay. Why? Wouldn't you?"

"Sometimes I think it's not as easy as taking a vote and fixing everything," Jasmine sighed. "What if there's no right and wrong or black and white, but just sides? Papa and Mama need to work. Our family can't survive otherwise."

Tala couldn't believe what she was hearing. "Yes, but what about the bigger picture? Workers' voices aren't being heard. Tatay says the field workers are disposable labor to the growers. The only way things will change is to fight."

Tala stopped to take a breath, then looked at Jasmine beseechingly. "That's what everyone is trying to do with the strike. The workers just want to be seen and heard and taken seriously."

Jasmine had given up on swinging by now. "And my family just wants food on the table," she said quietly, kicking at the gravel. "It just seems like there are no easy answers."

"Hola!"

Tala and Jasmine jumped at the greeting. A boy and a girl were walking toward Tala and Jasmine. *He looks familiar,* Tala thought.

The kids stopped in front of the swings. "Do your parents work in the grape vineyards?" the boy asked.

That must be where I've seen him before. "Practically everyone's parents work in the grape vineyards," Tala said cautiously.

"What's it to you?" Jasmine snapped.

The boy smiled and held up one hand in peace. "The NFWA is collecting grievances. Our papa wants to know everything the workers don't like so they know what to change."

The girl handed Tala and Jasmine a pamphlet. "Can you give these to your parents?"

"Change starts small, yeah?" the boy added. "Even we can make a difference."

Tala looked at the pamphlet. The front had the NFWA logo along with the word "HUELGA." Huelga looks similar to the Tagalog term welga, which means "strike."

Suddenly, it dawned on Tala where she'd seen the two kids before.

"You're César Chávez's kids!" Tala didn't mean for it to come out as an exclamation. She just didn't expect the leader of the NFWA to send his kids out to recruit people.

The boy grinned. "Two of them, at least. Give those pamphlets to your parents, yeah? The more we know, the more we can change." The kids turned to leave.

"Wait!" Tala called after them.

"Tala," Jasmine hissed. "What are you thinking?"

"Don't worry," Tala whispered. "I'm a reporter in training, remember? I just want to ask a couple more questions." Tala hopped off the swing and jogged over to the Chávez siblings.

"My name's Tala." She held out her hand to shake each kid's hand. "My dad is one of the AWOC leaders. How come you get to help out? Do you have, like, a junior version of the NFWA or something?"

The girl laughed, showing off some of her missing baby teeth. "No, we just help out with the little things like passing out flyers, addressing envelopes, licking stamps, that sort of thing. There's always room for more if you're interested. It frees up Papa to do what's important to him."

The boy tapped the back of Tala's pamphlet. "There's the main office's address. Stop by sometime. You can see how we run things."

Tala bounced on the balls of her feet in excitement, hugging the pamphlet to her chest. "Yeah. I'll bring my dad along."

"Perfect." The boy gave her a little salute before they turned to leave. "See you soon, Tala."

Chapter Eleven

September 21, 1965
Dear Diary,

Lola always says when you expect something amazing, you get amazing results. I think she just means we need to stay positive no matter what. Lola likes to talk in riddles sometimes and do something she calls "debating," but everyone else would call it "arguing." One of her favorite targets is Tatay. She baits him like a fishing hook and Tatay falls for it every time. Their debates can get heated. I don't know why Tatay even bothers to say anything other than "you're right. You're always right." It would save him a lot of time and trouble if he just accepted you can't win a debate with Lola. I know that and I'm only eleven.

Tala

"Are you going somewhere, Tatay?" Tala looked up from her homework and watched as he shuffled through some papers on the kitchen table.

"I have a meeting at the NFWA headquarters in town." He touched the top of his head and frowned. "Have you seen my . . .?"

"Sunglasses?" Tala finished the question she knew he was going to ask. "They're on the kitchen counter. Next to your car keys."

"Excellent." Tatay tugged on Tala's braid as he walked past. "My next question was going to be 'Where are my keys?' This is an important meeting. I need to make sure everything is perfect."

"Can I come with you?" Tala followed him into the entryway, lining up the reasons why she needed to go in her head in case he said no. She needed the mimeograph machine to copy her news articles. She wanted to see the difference between NFWA headquarters and Filipino Hall. She could tell he was distracted and might need her help.

"This is a business meeting, Nene, not a field trip," Tatay said as he put his keys in his pocket.

"I'm not going to just look around," Tala insisted. "I'm going to help."

A half smile crept onto Tatay's mouth. "And what do you think needs your help, Tala?"

"Everything," she said. "What you're trying to do is bigger than anything anyone has ever done before. Don't you need all the help you can get?"

"Yes, Nene, but there's only so much adults can do, let alone children. What do you have planned?"

"I can make coffee or pass out flyers." Tala ticked off each task on her fingers. "I'm good at writing. Maybe the AWOC and NFWA can use that somehow. I've already written some articles about the strike. Maybe they can help distribute them. What's important to you is important to me, Tatay. Let me come along."

"Well, since you put it that way"—Tatay leaned down to look Tala in the eyes—"hop in the car. But I want you on your best behavior. This isn't a game. You're not playing reporter."

"Of course, Tatay," Tala said. "Just give me one minute."

Tala ran into her room and grabbed her steno notebook so she could write down impressions for a story that was forming in her mind. *It's not playing reporter if you're a real reporter-in-training, is it?* After Tala grabbed her notebook, she met Tatay at the car. The air felt charged with electricity. She was in for an adventure. She could just feel it.

NFWA Headquarters was housed in a white stucco building on Albany Street. It was the west side of town where most of the Mexican and Filipino houses and businesses were.

Tala took in the sight as they approached the entrance. The windows of the building were completely covered with "Huelga" flyers, banners, and the NFWA coat of arms. When they reached the front door, Tatay didn't knock but walked right in.

Inside was just as cluttered as the front windows. Dusty desks were scattered all over the room. There were three mimeograph machines. A stack of stamped envelopes sat on the corner of one desk, ready to be stuffed and mailed out to possible supporters. The walls were wallpapered with maps to all the targeted ranches, picket instructions, and supporter phone numbers.

"Stay close to me, Tala," Tatay warned.

"Where else would I go?" she asked.

Tatay cracked his knowing half-smile again. "Where would you not go?"

"True," Tala admitted.

Tala tried to stay close to Tatay, but she soon found herself lost in her own thoughts. *Who knew that there was so much planning involved in a strike? You don't just show up holding a sign. Scouts find the vineyard crew locations. Protesters rotate out who pickets where. Group leaders talk to the cops if there's a problem. There's so much organization.*

Tala glanced at her father. He was still deep in conversation with someone. She drifted to the closest secretary. "Who does all this?" Tala motioned at the maps and list of instructions.

The secretary looked up from mimeographing flyers. "It's a united effort, but César's touch is on all of it."

"By united effort, do you mean Itliong and Chávez?" Tala asked.

The secretary gave a condescending smile. "Sometimes, but not always."

"Why not?" Tala pressed, choosing to ignore the woman's obvious disdain.

The secretary's smile faltered. "Why are you asking?"

Tala held up her steno pad. "I'm a reporter in training."

"César is a very busy man and can't always consult the AWOC on every little thing." The secretary chose her words carefully. "Everyone has a role to perform in the strike, Mr. Itliong included."

"We usually call him Manong Itliong because he was part of the first Filipino immigration to America," Tala said. "*Manong* means big brother. It's a term of respect."

"I'll keep that in mind." The secretary shuffled some papers around her desk, looking like she wanted to end the conversation.

Tala pressed on. "What's Chávez like?" she asked. "Based on the stories I've heard around the ranch, he seems to eat, breath, and sleep nothing but strike business."

"I can assure you he's just as human as the rest of us," she said. "His passion for the cause is truly inspiring, though, I'll give you that."

"I'd like to meet him," Tala said half to herself, not really expecting an answer. Now *that* would be a story if she got to meet the head of the NFWA in person.

"César is always on the go," the secretary said. "The only way to get to talk to him is to drive him to the strike sites. He has chronic back issues and driving can sometimes be too painful."

That gave Tala an idea. Now she just needed Tatay to agree to it.

WAYS FOR ALL AGES TO
HELP THE STRIKE

By Tala Mendoza

If your family is not striking or if you're too young to join the picket lines, you can help the strike effort in other ways. Try these ideas to boost your involvement in this important event:

- Cook or bake a meal for a striking family: Who doesn't like food? With no steady source of income, basic things like food and clothing can be hard for a strike worker to get. Sometimes the smallest gesture makes the biggest difference.
- Donate clothes: Look through your dresser and closet for clothes you no longer wear. Most workers have large families. Organize a clothing drive to help farmworker families in need.
- Pass out AWOC and NFWA flyers: Volunteering your time is just as important as cooking meals and donating clothes. If you're a kid, make sure your parents know where you're going and take a friend.

The strike is a community effort and now it can be a whole family effort. Delano should stand united, no matter what side of the picket line your family is on.

Chapter Twelve

September 24, 1965

Dear Diary,

Success! It took a lot of begging, a lot of pleading, and a lot of grumbling from Nanay, but I finally talked Tatay into taking me with him to the picket line. I want to be an investigative journalist. But how can a reporter, or even a reporter in training, report on anything if they're not in the thick of things?

Luckily, Tatay bought that argument, but made me promise to stay close to him at all times. I'd agree to do just about anything if it meant seeing the strike up close and being able to help out in any way I could.

The only thing that would make this better is if Jasmine could come with me. But I couldn't ask her. Her parents would never allow it.

Besides, we really haven't talked that much lately.

Tala

*T*ala woke to someone gently shaking her.

"Wake up, Nene," Tatay's voice was quiet.

Tala opened her eyes. Her room was dark.

"You need to get up and get ready if you want to come with me today," Tatay said, louder this time.

Tala groaned. "I'm up, I'm up. Just give me a few minutes."

Tala made quick work of getting ready, making sure to grab her steno notebook and a pencil before she came out for breakfast. After some breakfast, Tala and Tatay drove to the NFWA headquarters in town to meet up with the other picketers. By the time they pulled up, there were fifteen other cars waiting.

"We call it the picket caravan," Tatay said. "Are you sure you want to do this, Tala?"

She nodded. "I don't just want to hear about what's going on, Tatay, I want to be a part of it."

He sighed. "Now remember, while the protesters vow to be nonviolent, the growers might try and do something to intimidate us. Just stay close to me."

Tala stood on tiptoes when a group of people emerged from the NFWA headquarters. They were gathered around a Mexican man with thick, black hair wearing a button-up shirt. He pointed at a map in his hands, giving directions to the different ranches that were going to be picketed today.

It was César Chávez.

Even from where she stood next to Tatay's car, she could hear Chávez's quiet, confident voice. She'd heard that Chávez was a born leader. People said he wasn't the head of the NFWA just to be a figurehead. He believed in helping the common man. At home, Tala heard him called the "Mexican Larry Itliong." The men held similar positions in their unions and were no strangers to organizing strikes.

Watching Chávez maneuver his way through the crowd, Tala was taken by how different he was from Itliong. They fought for the same cause, but their personalities and presences were complete opposites. Chávez picked his words and actions carefully. Itliong was known for being a "tough guy."

"Ride with us, Señor Chávez!" Tala called before she could lose her nerve. Tatay's face turned red at the bold suggestion.

"Tala," he warned.

"I'm a reporter in training," she whispered back, knowing that it might make him angry but also knowing she needed to do something. "I'm following the story."

"Señor Chávez is a very busy man," Tatay said. "Don't bother him."

"No. No, it's no bother." Chávez spoke up. "I've seen you at the AWOC meeting and on the picket line. What is your name?"

"Danilo Mendoza," Tatay said, holding out his hand to shake Chávez's. "This very forward girl is my daughter

Tala. She thinks she's a reporter. She'll talk your ear off if given the chance."

"I *am* a reporter," Tala protested, shooting her dad a you're-embarrassing-me look. "Or will be when I grow up. I'm in training now. I mean, I like talking. I like learning more about people. And I want to make a difference with my writing, like Rachel Carson or . . ." Tala trailed off, realizing she had derailed a bit from her purpose. "Eh, I mean, can I interview you for a story?"

Chávez's eyes crinkled around the corners when he smiled. "I believe you will be the best reporter I've talked to this month." He motioned at the others to get in their cars and start the caravan before climbing into Tatay's car.

My plan worked! It actually worked!

Tala scrambled into the back seat. Chávez set a two-way radio in the middle of the front seat and gave Tatay brief directions to the first stop on the picket caravan. Then Chávez turned so he could see Tala over his shoulder.

"How long have you been a reporter?" Chávez asked. Chávez was treating her like she was a grown up and a real reporter.

"Two years," she said. "Ever since I wrote about keeping milk-and-graham-cracker snack time at school."

"It was a hard-hitting investigative piece," Tatay teased. "Give me graham crackers or give me death."

Chávez chuckled. "And how old are you now?"

"Eleven." The more she talked, the more confident Tala felt.

"When I was your age, I walked to school barefoot because we could not afford shoes," Chávez said quietly.

"We fished in the local canal and cut wild mustard greens to eat. Sometimes we traded eggs for goat's milk, flour, or meat. If we needed extra money, my brother and I would walk along the highway and pick up discarded cigarette packs. Once we collected enough, we'd sell the tinfoil lining."

"So you were born into the life of a farmworker?"

He nodded. "I know the fight—I know the life—firsthand."

Tala was silent for a moment. *I'm not sure why I thought he was above the farmworker struggles.*

"Did you graduate from high school?" Tala asked, knowing that most children of farmworkers, especially boys, never completed their education.

He shook his head. "My father had an accident so I went to work in the fields. I made it through the eighth grade. It wasn't so unusual back then. I studied on my own and am still learning every day. We fight for a better future. That's not something that is given to us. It's something we earn."

He stopped for a breath, and for once, Tala was all out of words.

Before Tala could think of something to say, Chávez looked back at Tala and said, "You talk about women journalists making a difference. Did you know that a woman founded the NFWA with me?"

Tala shook her head no, and he continued. "Her name is Dolores Huerta, but not many people know about her. We share a common goal of improving farmworker lives. Dolores negotiates all the contracts between the growers and workers."

"I had no idea," Tala said.

Chávez nodded. "They may want to see my face on the news, but it's Dolores they talk to to settle matters."

Just then, Tatay stopped the car. They were on a dusty road and had pulled up beside a foreman's truck. Tala had so completely lost track of time, that she didn't know how long they'd been driving or which ranch they were at. She saw a small group of workers in the fields. They looked up when the strike caravan stopped but quickly looked away when the foreman barked at them to ignore the protesters.

"We're going on to the next site," someone's voice crackled across the two-way radio. "I'll take half."

"We'll stay here," Chávez said into the radio, and then nodded at Tatay. Tatay turned off the engine. Tala watched as the back half of the caravan drove away.

Chávez got out of the car and Tala started to as well, but froze with her on the handle. "Tatay?" Tala asked. "What are the cops doing here?"

"Don't worry, Nene," he said. "They're here to make sure we don't cause trouble. And we aren't planning on it."

"Are you sure?"

Tatay nodded and tugged one of Tala's braids. "Just think, if anything does happen, it will make a great story." He winked.

Tala climbed out of the car. She knew that the strike leaders had to bring in strikers from other areas because so many farmworkers had returned to the fields. But she wasn't prepared for the number of protesters she saw. There were Filipinos and Mexicans alongside one another, as well as hippies and anti-war protesters. The motley group was already lining up facing the field, holding signs with the NFWA logo or "huelga" scrawled across a plain background. Chants of "we shall overcome" mingled with chants of "huelga." The vineyard foreman cranked up his radio to try to drown out the protesters.

"Don't look at them!" he commanded his field crew. "You're here to work, not fraternize!"

Two of the field workers broke from their row and ran across the street to the protesters. They talked rapidly in Spanish with Chávez and someone who looked like he could be a strike leader. The strike leader handed the workers some pamphlets. The workers looked back and forth between the field and picket line before stepping up to join the protesters. One crumpled up his pamphlet and threw it at the foreman.

"No throwing things!" One of the cops walked over to the strike leader. "Tell him he can't do that. All the foreman saw was something being thrown. How does he know it's not a rock? No throwing things, not even paper."

"Yes, sir," the strike leader said. "Remember your vow!" he called loudly enough for everyone to hear. "Everyone agreed to be nonviolent. There's no place for you in this movement if you can't remember that."

The line of protesters murmured they understood.

Tatay and Tala stayed with the protestors the entire day. When the foreman at the first site moved his crew into the middle of the field, the strike caravan moved on to the next site. Protestors chanted and held up signs. No matter where the strikers went, the police silently followed behind to ensure the peaceful protest remained peaceful. It did.

September 25, 1965
Dear Diary,

What a day! I can't exactly say picketing itself is exciting, but being able to finally stand next to Tatay to show my support in everything he and the other workers are going through IS exciting.

And the best part? I got to interview César Chávez today! He was very kind to me when he really didn't have to be. He answered all my questions and took me seriously. He didn't seem to mind that I'm a reporter in training, unlike some other people I've talked to before.

I just wish Manong Itliong was there today. I could have interviewed both my heroes! (Well, Tatay is my hero, too, but I can talk to him all the time.) I admire Itliong's fire. I feel the same fire inside me. We're both passionate about helping people, just in different ways. If I can keep the fire for writing burning as long as Itliong has kept his fire for organizing farmworkers burning, I'll be very happy.

Time for bed. It's been a long day!

Tala

Chapter Thirteen

September 26, 1965

Dear Diary,

Reporters are not supposed to take sides. It's called being objective. But how can I be objective when all my friends and family are affected in one way or another because of the strike?

Jasmine's family is bullied constantly because they broke the picket line. Just yesterday, Jasmine found the word "scab" written across her locker. Again. That's the fifth time in two weeks we've had to scrub her locker clean. The strikers are supposed to take a vow of nonviolence but not all strikers honor it. And the growers don't either. But just because you don't agree with someone, doesn't mean you can treat them the way people are treating Jasmine's family.

The longer the strike goes on, the more it seems like there's no in-between. There's no way to stay objective. I try to report "just the facts" when I write an article, but even that seems somehow not good enough. There's no passion when you're reporting facts and figures. Maybe that's the problem, though. People have too much passion about the subject and that's what gets them carried away. Passion makes strike supporters slingshot four thousand marbles at the field workers. Passion makes growers tear signs out of the hands of protesters and blast the signs apart with a shotgun. Passion makes someone run a strike scout off the road when they're driving around looking for open ranches. Passion makes strike supporters light grape boxes on fire in front of the police station.

This strike is dividing us because we're not able to see the other side's perspective. I'm worried about what the divide is doing to Nanay, Tatay, and me. Jasmine and me too. I feel like it's pulling my best friend and me farther and farther apart.

Tatay and the unions say they are fighting for a better life. Maybe some people see that as wrong, but I think those same people might just be scared of what's different. Field workers have endured injustice for a long time. Now people come in trying to change all that? I'd be scared too. I AM scared.

Tala

GRAPE WORKERS SAY IT'S TIME FOR CHANGE

By Tala Mendoza

Growing grapes is big business in Delano. While most farm labor can be done with the help of machines, wine and table grapes are one of the few crops that need a human touch ten months out of the year.

A machine can't spray, trim, and girdle the various grapevines grown in the vineyard. Workers know the difference between Cardinal, Thompson, Ribier, Red Malaga, Emperor, Almerias, Calmerias, and Muscat grapes.

Workers know how to check the size and color of the grapes, size of the bunch, and to trim any bad grapes before packing. A machine can't do that, either.

With their labor, time, and attention so needed, why do grape workers only earn $1,378.00 a year? With just a 20-cent increase per hour from $1.20 to $1.40, workers may not need charity assistance just to clothe and feed their families.

Workers say it's time for a change. Do you agree?

Chapter Fourteen

*T*atay burst into the kitchen where Tala sat doing her homework and Nanay was baking bread.

"Our wages are being increased." Tatay had a wide smile as he waved a piece of paper in his hand. "They're offering an extra five cents an hour."

"Good." Nanay kneaded the dough like she was mad at it. "That means you can go back to work."

"No, it means we're being effective," Tatay said. "Besides, we didn't ask for a five-cent increase, we asked for twenty cents. If we accept five, what message is that going to send?"

"It will send the message that the AWOC and NFWA care about people's jobs," Nanay said. "How is keeping people out of work effective?"

"We're not keeping anyone out of work who doesn't want to be." Tatay crumpled up the paper from the growers and threw it away. "Besides, we talked about this."

Nanay slammed her fists into the doughy ball. "No. We didn't talk about this, Danilo. You talked about this with your AWOC friends but not with me. Maybe you talked to me before the strike vote, but since then I might as well be invisible in any decisions that affect this family." She stopped her kneading and flung a floured hand out in Tala's direction. "What sort of message does that give to Tala? We're supposed to be partners, Danilo, but ever since the strike, your partners are the AWOC and NFWA . . . not me."

"This is bigger than you or me," Tatay insisted. "What we're trying to do will change our lives and everyone's lives forever. We can't be content to just sit back and watch the world go by anymore. Change doesn't happen by sitting still."

"Change, change, change. All you talk about is change," Nanay snapped back.

It was the same argument they had been having since the strike started. No matter how many times Tala heard it, it still upset her to see her parents so unhappy. She escaped to her bedroom.

Tala climbed onto her bed and tried to drown out the sound with her pillow. She tried to imagine this new world Tatay spoke of. *Would things really be better if workers suddenly earned twenty cents more an hour? Would that fix the problems inside the homes or just the problems on the outside?*

Tala sat up when she heard the door open. It was Lola.

Lola smiled as she sat down next to Tala and put her arm around her granddaughter. "I know you're worried, Nene, but you know it's just words in there between your parents, right? There's no action behind them."

"Rosie Cruz's parents fought over the strike and her mom left," Tala said. "What if Nanay does the same thing?"

"No, Tala, she won't," Lola said softly. "Your mother is fiery. She always has been. You have some of her fire too."

"I hope so."

Lola winked at me. "I know so."

Tala turned to look out the window. Maybe Lola was right. Tala hoped she could put her fire and passion to good use someday. *I don't want to be just a great reporter, I want to write about greatness.*

LARRY ITLIONG JOINED FIRST STRIKE AS TEEN

By Tala Mendoza

Sixteen. Most sixteen-year-olds are worried about school, friends, sports, and a part-time job. When Larry Itliong was sixteen, he had already moved halfway across the world from the Philippines to the United States. Sixteen was also the age he joined his first strike. By the time World War II ended, Itliong had established unions in Alaska, Washington, Montana, South Dakota, and California. He brought his dedication to the leadership position of the Agricultural Workers Organizing Committee. The Delano Grape Strike workers are fortunate to have such an experienced leader in their corner.

PART II
1966

Chapter Fifteen

The AWOC and NFWA set out a plan for the strike. They targeted over thirty growers and ranchers, rotating which ranches they picketed each day. In the early days of the strike, growers beat up picketers, kicked dirt in their faces, sprayed pesticide on them, and shot at protestors' signs.

The organizations started a fund to help cover the picketers' lost wages. As the strike continued into months four, five, and six, there were un-picketed "safety valve" ranches where workers could get a day's or week's worth of work (and pay) before rejoining the strike.

The strikers persisted but didn't see much change.

MARCH FOR DELANO GRAPE STRIKE PLANNED

By Tala Mendoza

The 1965 strikes in Sacramento and Coachella are over, but the Delano Grape Strike is not. Delano workers aren't willing to settle for the small wage increase offered by the growers. They want all their demands, including wage increases, better working conditions, and—most importantly—a contract met.

After Schenley, a big grower in Delano, sprayed strikers with agricultural poison, the NFWA decided it was time to take action. César Chávez has organized a march from Delano to Sacramento in protest. It will start on March 17 and is expected to end on April 10.

Will this be the act that incites the growers to change? Only time will tell.

March 17, 1966

Dear Diary,

I wish I were older so I could go with Tatay on the march to Sacramento. But the march is 300 miles long and will take several weeks, so I am not allowed.

There are a lot of jobs to do related to the march. Tatay says it takes a lot of planning and organization to make something look so effortless. There are people who scout locations along the route so the marchers have places to stay, people who arrange meals, people who drive the luggage truck, and even someone to drive the portable toilet truck. If I was allowed to help, I wouldn't care what role I had. I'd even drive the portable toilet truck just to be a part of it! But I guess I'm going to focus on doing what I can: writing about it.

Do you remember when I thought my life was boring? Hey naku, was I wrong!!

Tala

On the morning of March 17, Main Street in downtown Delano was bustling. People were everywhere. Police. Strike supporters. Grower supporters. Newspaper reporters. TV news reporters with video cameras rolling. All for the farmworkers' strike.

"You know you don't have a permit to march down Main Street." The police chief got out of his car and stared down Chávez and the other leaders. "Take this sideshow back the way you originally planned."

"This is a pilgrimage, not a demonstration or sideshow." Chávez leaned against his "Huelga" sign. "The sidewalk is public property."

"But the street's not," the chief said. "You're creating a public safety hazard."

"It's only our families wanting to say goodbye," Larry Itliong said. "After that, we'll be on our way."

The chief didn't answer right away. He watched the TV news cameras rolling. He seemed nervous, as if he didn't want to make the wrong move and look like the bad guy for all the world to see. "Say your goodbyes and move it along," he said.

Everyone breathed a sigh of relief. Tala, who was there with Tatay, Nanay, and Lola, didn't know she was even holding her breath until it all came out in a whoosh.

"Did you remember to dress in layers?" Nanay checked and double-checked Tatay's shirt, flannel, and jacket as if fussing with his shirt buttons would make him stay longer. A day without Tatay seemed unheard of, let alone a month.

"Yes, oyab." Tatay pulled a chain out from under his shirt. "I have your Saint Christopher medal for safe travels, as well."

"Don't take Saint Christopher off." Nanay clutched the sides of his open flannel shirt until her knuckles turned white. "Come home safe."

Tatay nodded toward the crowd and TV crews. "With this many witnesses along the route, no one will try anything."

"You still need to be careful." Tala could see the tears forming in the corners of her mother's eyes.

Tatay leaned over to kiss his wife's forehead. "I will. I promise."

Next it was Tala's turn.

"Do you promise to write every day?" she asked.

Tatay tugged her braid. "I can't promise every day, but I'll write as much as I can. All you have to do is turn on the TV, Nene, to know I'm fine and thinking of you."

"I wish I could go with you."

"You need to stay home and take care of your mother. Can you do that for me?" he asked. "Can you be strong for Nanay and Lola? It'll only be a few weeks but it will feel like a lifetime."

Tala nodded. "Write when you can and tell me everything."

Tatay smiled before grabbing Tala in a tight hug. He kissed the top of her head before letting go. "Adyos."

As Tatay took his spot next to the other marchers, someone started singing "We Shall Overcome" and everyone joined in. With one last look at the families they were leaving behind, the AWOC, NFWA, and their supporters started walking straight down Main Street.

Tala waved until the last marcher was only a speck in the distance. "Adyos, Tatay. Adyos."

Chapter Sixteen

March 24, 1966

Dear Diary,

I know Mama means well and thinks she's protecting me, but I wish when she said "no being friends with strike kids," she didn't lump Tala into the mix. Yes, Tala's family is involved in the strike, but I know her nanay doesn't like it any more than my mama does. They can agree on that, right? Why can't they agree on letting us be friends? Tala's nanay doesn't say who she can or cannot be friends with. Why does mine?

I know Mama worries about me. She worries about those strike kids that write "scab" on my locker or throw food at me at lunch. But Tala isn't throwing food or writing stuff on my locker. If anything, she tries to protect me. Mama only sees a strike kid, and to her, strike kid equals bad news. It hurts to pull away from Tala, but what Mama says goes in this house. I need to obey . . . no matter how much it hurts.

I try to talk only about school work when we're together. I make up excuses why I can't go to her house after school. I know Tala is confused—I can see it written all over her face—but I don't know what else to do. Is it better to fade away slowly than disappear all at once? Either way, it doesn't make me miss Tala any less. I want my best friend back. But I don't think that can happen until the strike is over.

Jasmine

"It feels like I've barely seen you in six months," Tala said. She was sitting with Jasmine on the swings outside Tala's apartment. It was quiet for once. The march was still going on and the strikers who stayed behind hadn't targeted this ranch in a while.

Jasmine looked everywhere but at Tala. With her hunched shoulders and faraway eyes, she looked sad. She shrugged. "Mama doesn't like me playing with strike kids."

Tala sucked in her breath. "Is that what you think of me now?"

She shook her head so hard her twin braids hit her face. "No, but I have to listen to Mama. She's just trying to keep us safe."

"The strike is nonviolent," Tala said. "It always has been. Those people who call you names at church and write *scab* on your locker aren't following the rules. They're not part of the unions."

"I know that, but you know how Mama worries." Jasmine wrapped her braid around her finger before unwinding it. Tala watched as she did that six times. *Wind, unwind. Wind, unwind.*

"Is there something else to worry about, Jasmine?" She wasn't telling the whole truth. Tala knew it as surely as she felt her friend's sadness.

Jasmine paused, considering the question. Finally she said, "Someone lit grape boxes on fire in front of our house last week. They strung up a dummy from the tree and wrote *scab* across its chest." She looked at Tala with tears in her eyes. "Mama's scared, Tala. So am I."

Tala's hand flew up to her mouth. "Oh no! How come you didn't tell me sooner?"

Jasmine shrugged.

"It's just some people taking advantage of the strike to scare you," Tala reached out and squeezed Jasmine's hand to show support. "They won't actually *do* anything."

"How do you know that?" she whispered. "How do you know they're going to stop at dummies and grape boxes? What if Papa or one of my brothers is next?"

"They wouldn't do that," Tala insisted.

"But how do you know that?" Jasmine's voice trembled. Her hand shook when she raised it to her mouth. "You don't know what anyone will do until they do it." Jasmine swiped at a tear on her cheek and looked away to compose herself. After taking a deep breath, she looked back at Tala and said, "We're moving. After school is out in May, we're out of Delano."

Tala was speechless for a beat. "Moving?" she finally managed. The news was Tala's worst nightmare come true. "I thought your father decided to stay in Delano. We've always been together, Jasmine. I don't know what to do without you. You're like the sister I never had."

Jasmine tried to smile but her mouth shook too much to keep it up for long. "I'll write. We still have two months before school is out. That's plenty of time to make memories."

"But they'll all be touched with sadness." Tala squeezed Jasmine's hands tighter. "There's no changing your parents' minds?"

Jasmine shook her head no. "Papa knows a foreman down in Coachella. We'll go there first."

"Coachella?" Tala repeated. "That's four hours away. You might as well move to the moon."

The girls sat in silence until Mr. Perez's car pulled up. It was time for Jasmine to go home.

"There's Papa," Jasmine said, getting up from her spot on the swing. She looked back over her shoulder at Tala, "Don't be mad. I would stay if it was up to me."

"I'm not mad. I just wish things could change faster so you didn't have to go." Tala watched as Jasmine climbed into the back seat of the car, then waved.

Tala got up to head home. She took a deep breath of resolve, trying to push her sadness and anger away. She didn't want Nanay and Lola to worry. The strike had finally provided her with her first real test of strength: her best friend was leaving.

Chapter Seventeen

March 25, 1966
Road to Sacramento
Dear Tala,

I wish you were here with me to see what I see.
It's one thing to hear about the support people
give us marchers, but it's completely different
to see it and feel the energy from all these
strangers supporting our cause. They came out
along the route to let us know we matter, Tala.
We matter.

   When we set out on this journey we called
it a pilgrimage. The more we walk under the
banner of the Our Lady of Guadalupe, the more
I believe it. A little girl gave me a cross made
out of a palm frond on Palm Sunday. I looked
down at it and thought if I can make the life of

just one child better, it will be worth it. *I hope the one child's life that I change is yours, Nene.*

There's a lot of time to think when you walk everywhere. If I think about you, your Nanay and Lola too much, I get homesick. My mind won't shut off at night, though. I look up at the stars and pray I am doing the honorable thing. I want to build a world where you don't have to work the fields just because our family has done so for generations. If you do choose the fields, I want it to be a safe, fair place for you to work. Your nanay doesn't always agree with me or my ideals, but I know you understand, Tala. You can see the world I'm trying to help create. I'm grateful for your support.

We should arrive in Sacramento for Easter. Turn on Lola's TV after you read this and think of me. Know that I'll be thinking of you.

Your loving tatay

MARCH TO SACRAMENTO ENDS ON EASTER SUNDAY

By Tala Mendoza

Ten thousand people gathered in Sacramento to witness the end of the 26-day march from Delano. Once the marchers reached the park at the center of the city, Chávez stepped forward. He read a plan for Delano. He said, "We are suffering, we shall unite, we shall strike, we shall overcome. Our pilgrimage is the match that will light our cause for all farmworkers to see what is happening here, so that they may do as we have done." The crowd erupted in cheers and whistles, calling "Viva la huelga!" Viva la huelga!

Chapter Eighteen

August 23, 1966

Dear Jasmine,

It seems weird to have to write you a letter. How is Coachella? Did your papa get the job he wanted?

Last week, I rode my bike by your old house. Even though I knew a new family lived there, I almost stopped. I've done this a couple times. I've decided I won't go into town because I don't want to be reminded that you aren't there.

School is just as bad. Nanay told me I should find a new best friend. I told her that was impossible. There's no replacing you.

Write me when you can and tell me all about Coachella. Most of all, don't forget me!

Your best friend forever,
Tala

BREAKING NEWS: NFWA AND AWOC MERGE TO FORM UFW

By Tala Mendoza

The NFWA and AWOC have combined to form the United Farm Workers Organizing Committee, or UFW. After working together for almost a year with the same goals and guidelines, it makes sense for the unions to merge.

The strike continues with no end in sight.

August 26, 1966
Dear Tala,

Coachella is like Delano, only bigger! I keep looking around, expecting you to be here. My new school is big. I feel like I can get lost just by walking through the doors. The kids are mostly friendly, but no one can replace you as my best friend.

You know I'm not very good at writing. If I could cook you a meal and put all my thoughts and feelings into that, I would. Don't forget about me, Tala. Never, ever, ever.

Jasmine

September 1, 1966
Dear Jasmine,

Did you realize that this year is the first year we've spent our birthdays apart? Can you believe that? I want to write the ONLY time instead of the FIRST time, because I won't let you just drift away from me, Jasmine. Promise me next year we'll be together for our birthdays. Even if I have to take a train to Coachella or we meet halfway, I won't let another birthday go by without you. I promise. Pinkie swear?

The next time you write, tell me all about your new school. Don't worry about talking about your new friends. I don't mind. I'll just pretend I'm there with you.

Tala

September 1, 1966
Dear Diary,

Lola made me a cupcake for my birthday because it takes less flour and other ingredients. I don't think she even used eggs. Lola and Nanay are becoming masters at making a little stretch a long way. We all are. I don't blame the strike for forcing us to make do with so little. I know what the workers are fighting for is important.

   Life is really different than it was one year ago. We wake up with the sun and go to bed when it sets to save on the electric bill. We eat rice with every meal. We live off of union strike funds, our savings, and anything Tatay and Nanay can make when they work the safety valve ranches for a week here, a week there. But it never seems like enough. We don't have a car anymore. I don't go to Mr. Mendoza's store anymore, either. He finally told Nanay and Tatay that they had to pay off their bill before they could buy from him again. And going there for the free penny candy doesn't seem right after all that. It's probably just as well anyway; it doesn't seem right without Jasmine.

I don't think anyone knew the strike would last as long as it has. It could be over tomorrow or a week from now. It might even last another whole year. We just don't know, and that's the worst part. How can you prepare for something that cannot be predicted?

Tala

September 10, 1966
Dear Tala,

Since you asked, I'll try to describe my school.
I don't know if I'd call any of the other kids
my friends. I don't mean they make fun of me
or anything like that. I don't eat lunch alone,
so don't worry about that either. I just mean
I'm still the new girl so people treat me like
I'm a little on the outside of the crowd. Maybe
they're used to seeing farm kids come and go
with the harvest, so they don't want to get
too close. I think we'd do the same. Maybe
we did and didn't know we were treating the
migrant kids like temporary people instead of
someone worth getting to know. How's that
for a deep thought? I didn't know I had it in
me.

My school is so big I can go all day
without seeing any of my brothers or sisters.
People don't even ask if I'm "Isko's sister" or

"Amala's sister." I'm just me. I could get used to that. The classes are a lot bigger than in Delano. Sometimes I raise my hand to answer questions. I'm never called on if I don't. There's always someone there with their hand up in the air to take the pressure off the rest of us. I like that part.

There's a group of girls in my grade that call themselves the Gatas. I haven't figured out why yet, but they're popular. Everyone wants to be part of the Gatas. I don't need a group to run around with. I do my best to avoid them.

Coachella and everything about it is new and different, but not in a bad way. Sometimes I feel like it's the first step to all those bigger and better things you wished for me. Remember that? You wished to be an investigative reporter and you said I'd be a big-city chef someday. Coachella feels like the first step on that road.

Write when you can! Tell me what's going on with the strike. I bet you know a lot more than the news reporters. They just keep saying the same stuff day after day. I can see Larry Itliong in the background on the evening news but he's never the one doing the talking—it's always César Chávez. Papa says the TV and newspaper reporters will find another story soon and then everyone will forget about Delano and the strike. Is the UFW planning anything big?

Your friend forever,
Jasmine

Chapter Nineteen

*N*anay stormed into the kitchen and angrily opened the cupboard. "UFW business? UFW business on a day of rest?" Nanay muttered, slamming the door after seeing it was nearly empty of food.

Tala had followed her in from the living room. "It's okay, Nanay," Tala said.

Nanay didn't seem to hear Tala. She continued her tirade. "Of course he has business when we have errands to do. He'd do anything to get out of coming along."

"I'll come along," Tala volunteered. "Are we going to the food bank?"

"It's closed on Sunday," Nanay said. "We're going to the real grocery store. Let's see if they'll let us buy on credit there."

"I'll get changed now," Tala said, and hurried to change out of her church clothes.

"At least there's a nice breeze in the air today," Tala said as they waited for the bus.

"Hmph," was all that Nanay could manage.

As the bus pulled up to the store, Tala spotted a group of protestors picketing out front.

"I can't even go to the store without hearing about this strike," Nanay grumbled.

"Wait. Is that Tatay?" Tala asked. "It is! It is Tatay!" He was holding a "Boycott Grapes" sign and walking in a circle with the other protesters. Tala bounded off the bus stairs to see him.

"Tatay!" she exclaimed. "What are you doing here? Nanay said you had UFW business."

"This *is* UFW business, Nene." He set down his picket sign and stepped out of the group to talk to Tala. "It's the next stage of the strike. We're moving to an all-out grape boycott."

"And how exactly is that going to make the growers want to meet your demands?" Nanay asked, crossing her arms over her chest and tapping her foot.

Tala jumped; she hadn't realized Nanay was there.

Tatay reached out to put his hand on Nanay's shoulder. "If people don't buy Delano grapes, it's either negotiate with the UFW or ruin your business. The choice is theirs."

A flashbulb suddenly went off in Tala's face. When her eyes cleared, she saw a reporter standing in front of her.

"I'm doing a story on a child's perspective of the strike. Care to give me some quotes?" the reporter talked quickly.

"Sure." There was no way Tala would give up the chance to talk to a real reporter. A real *female* reporter. Tala could hardly contain her excitement. "What do you want to know?" Tala asked.

"Are your parents involved in the strike and boycott?" The reporter took out a steno notepad to write down what Tala said.

"My tatay—I mean, dad—is, but it has affected my whole family." *And friends*, Tala thought. Then she added, "I support the strike by writing news articles. I distribute them at church and school. People seem to like them. At least I haven't found too many in the trash." Tala laughed nervously. "People say my articles keep them informed."

"That's great! How inventive of you," the reporter said. "How has your life changed since the strike?"

Tala figured the reporter wanted her to say something about how they didn't use much electricity because the bill was too high, took cold showers instead of hot, and ate rice and beans most nights, but she didn't want to talk about the sacrifices. She wanted to talk about what she learned since the strike began.

"I'm more aware of everything going on around me," Tala answered. "I don't take anything for granted. There are people suffering. I'm part of those people."

A look of confusion at the unanswered question flashed across the reporter's face, but she quickly recovered. "If you could suggest one thing to help end the strike, what would it be?"

"I'd ask the growers to talk to the UFW," Tala said. "Tatay says the growers act like they're the only ones suffering, but we've been suffering for generations. He says it's time for a change. The growers can help that or hurt that. The choice is up to them."

"Well, aren't you wise beyond your years," the reporter marveled. She thanked Tala for her time, handed Tala her business card in case she thought of anything else she wanted to tell her, and moved on.

Tala wasn't sure if her words were good enough to make it into the article, but she spoke the truth. That was all anyone could ask of her.

PART III

Fall 1967

Chapter Twenty

By boycotting Delano grapes, the UFW took their fight from the fields to the dinner table. The union sent striking workers all over the United States and Canada to talk about their experiences. They felt if people could see, hear, and talk to the affected field workers instead of just watching the TV news, support for the cause would grow. They were right. Soon, the boycott went international. The growers may not have been willing to listen to the plight of the workers, but the world was.

September 1, 1967
Dear Diary,

I can't believe I'm thirteen today! A teenager! Hay naku!
In some ways it seems like a lifetime ago when Isko gave
me this diary for my eleventh birthday.

If anyone had told me two years ago everything
that would happen from then to now, I wouldn't
have believed them. I still have trouble believing all
that I've seen in such a short time. The strike, the
boycott, Jasmine moving away . . .

Sometimes I wish I could rewind time and make
it stand still. Other times, I know the only way to
learn is to go forward.

Tala

"*T*ala!?" Jasmine squealed. "Is it really you?"

"Yes," Tala laughed, twisting the phone cord around her finger. "Happy birthday! I haven't talked to you in so long."

"I know," Jasmine agreed. "Too long."

"So how are you? How do you like Coachella?" Tala asked.

"I'm okay," Jasmine said. "Coachella is better than I thought it would be." She paused. "It's quiet. Delano is never quiet."

"It used to be, remember?" Tala asked. "We used to say nothing at all happened in Delano. People didn't even stop when they drove through. They forgot about us. Now no one can forget about us."

"But don't you think it's kind of like a sideshow now?" Jasmine asked. "That's what Papa says, at least. The TV cameras. The out-of-town newspaper reporters. First the strike, now the boycott."

"Tatay says the only reason the UFW needs to get the attention of TV and news reporters is because the growers think if they ignore the problem it will go away," Tala said. "He says looking the other direction won't make wages or working conditions better. All it does is delay the inevitable. It's like putting a Band-Aid on your finger when you catch it in the grape-sorting machine. The Band-Aid isn't going to stop you needing stitches. The growers ignoring us isn't going to stop us from spreading the word."

Jasmine started to say something and then was silent.

"What?" Tala managed to sound curious instead of angry. "What is it, Jasmine? If you want to say something, just say it."

"You always make it sound like *you* are part of the strike." Jasmine sounded annoyed. "You have since it first started. 'The growers don't take *us* seriously. *We're* fighting for what's right. Ignoring *us* won't make the problem go away.' You're not part of the union, Tala. It's not your fight."

Tala's stomach dropped to her feet. *Is this how Jasmine really feels? Does Jasmine really think I am just some silly kid caught up in a cause that isn't my own? Does she think I am*

playing at writing articles instead of believing in what Tatay and the rest of the UFW stand for?

"It's not some kid's game to me." Tala's voice shook when she was finally able to speak. "It's real, Jasmine."

"Your tatay is in the UFW, Tala, not you," Jasmine said quietly.

"Do you really think I'm playing at this?" Tala blinked hard several times, trying her best to hold in tears. "Why would I do that?"

"Because you said yourself your life—our lives— were boring before the strike," Jasmine said. "You needed something to grab on to, to report on, and that just happened to be the strike. It could have been anything, really. Remember your graham cracker and milk exposé? You find a cause and throw yourself into it. The strike isn't your fight, though. Not really."

There were a million things Tala could have said in that moment to hurt Jasmine like she hurt her. Instead, all she said was "Hey, Jasmine? Happy birthday to us." Then she hung up the phone.

EPILOGUE

Chapter Twenty-One

The Delano Grape Strike and table grape boycott lasted another three years. In 1968, some members of the UFW thought they should use violence as a way to get the message across and be heard. César Chávez fasted for twenty-five days in February to re-dedicate the movement to the message of nonviolence. He lost thirty-five pounds during the hunger strike, but the idea of taking personal responsibility for any talk of violence in the group and leading by example worked. The UFW also knew that people all over the US wanted to help their cause but couldn't drop everything and come stand in a picket line. That's where the table grape boycott came in. Anyone could "help" by not buying Delano grapes. The boycott cost the growers over seventeen million dollars in profit.

Before the Delano strike, workers had tried for over forty years to unionize. Their efforts never worked. In 1970, five years after the strike began, the growers and workers signed a lasting agreement for better wages, working conditions, and benefits.

In 1971, Larry Itliong resigned from the UFW over a disagreement with Chávez. He felt the union wasn't supporting aging Filipino workers. Itliong was a delegate at the 1972 Democratic National Convention and founded a retirement home for UFW workers called Agbayani Village. Even though he left the UFW, he continued to support and help organize strikes, such as the 1974 Safeway Supermarket Strike. He fought tirelessly for farmworker and Filipino rights.

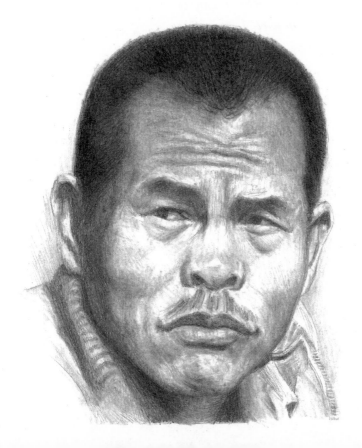

September 8, 1975
Dear Diary,

It feels strange but at the same time comforting to look back through these pages. Remember when I said I wondered where I'd be in ten years? Well, here I am.

Sometimes I ask myself "If I knew then what I know now, would I still do it?" Would I still believe in the strike so wholeheartedly that it almost ruined my friendship with Jasmine? As much as I want to say "no," the only answer I can give is "yes."

The strike ended in 1970 and Jasmine's family moved back to Delano. We graduated high school together and even moved to the same town to attend college. We're the first two in our families to go to college. Isko followed his brothers into the grape fields. He's still the fastest grape girdler around. I don't work the fields anymore. I'm too busy with school. This spring, Jasmine graduates from culinary school and I graduate from Cal State with a journalism degree. Isko's not so annoying anymore either . . . but I'd never say that to his face! Nanay still thinks it would be wonderful if Isko and I get married someday. I think there's so much more life for me to explore before I even think of getting married to Isko or anyone else. At least now I know I don't have to pick between a career or family. I can have both.

As I look ahead to the next chapters in my life, I'm never going to forget how Tatay and the rest of the UFW fought so hard and so long for me to have a chance at becoming what I always dreamed of.

Tala

Author's Note

This is a work of fiction, but the Delano Grape Strike, several key players (Larry Itliong and César Chávez), and all events directly relating to the strike are true. I am completely indebted to the work of reporter and author John Gregory Dunne. He was embedded in Delano during the strike and experienced firsthand the struggles of both sides—workers and growers. He also interviewed many people multiple times. He, like a lot of reporters, seemed to be fascinated with the emerging face of the movement, César Chávez, but did not interview Larry Itliong extensively. I found Dunne's physical descriptions of Chávez, Itliong, Filipino Hall, and the NFWA headquarters particularly useful in describing Delano in the 1960s. All scenes that include Chávez and Itliong are accurate representations based on Dunne's reporting. This includes:

- The AWOC meeting where the members voted to strike. AWOC had talked about striking, but Itliong warned workers about the realities they would face if they went on strike. Itliong had been involved in strikes and unions since he was sixteen years old. He did not take voting to strike lightly. After thinking over the warnings, AWOC members called an emergency meeting the next night and voted "yes" to a strike.

• How AWOC and NFWA came together to strike. Both AWOC and NFWA intended to strike in Delano, but the AWOC was first to vote. The NFWA intended to strike in 1968, and were stockpiling money to pay striking workers in anticipation of this. Itliong knew NFWA needed to join with AWOC in order for the strike to be successful. So he went to Chávez to ask them to join. Traditionally, the growers had pitted the two groups against one other. If the predominantly Filipino AWOC called a strike, the mostly Mexican NFWA would scab the strike, and vice versa. The Delano Grape Strike was the first time both groups came together, and it was Itliong who brought them together.

• Tala's interview with César Chávez. The story of Chávez's childhood is true; I found it in John Gregory Dunne's interviews and book. The scene where Tatay chauffeurs Chávez to the picket site is also based on a real event. When Dunne was first sent to Delano to cover the strike, he noticed that Chávez was always on the go. One of the NFWA members told him "the only way to interview Chávez right now is to be his chauffeur." So he drove Chávez to the picket sites, just like Tatay does in the book.

- The Chávez kids helping pass out strike and NFWA flyers and pamphlets. Chávez's kids really did this! This was an easy way for the older kids to help out.

- The March to Sacramento. One hundred people originally signed up for the March to Sacramento. Dunne made it clear that only men were allowed to participate in the march, but didn't explain why. Anyone with health issues were disqualified. Supporters lined the roads along the route to show their support. Some even joined the march. The march itself and the TV news coverage brought a lot of awareness to the strike.

The biggest thing that struck me about the grape strike is that it was started by the Delano branch of AWOC. That branch consisted of mostly Filipino Americans led by

Larry Itliong. It was Itliong who convinced César Chávez and the NFWA to join them. It was Itliong who was the spark that lit the movement, even though he soon became eclipsed by the face of the movement, Chávez. Sadly, not all resources about the strike acknowledge Itliong's role. I tried to change that with this book. I tried to give Larry Itliong the recognition he deserves. I hope I was able to do that successfully. In 2015, California signed "Larry Itliong Day" into law. His birthday, October 25, is now a state holiday.

Though I researched extensively everything from Filipino culture to firsthand accounts of the strike for this book, I want to take the time to highlight some of my favorite sources. Please check these out if you're interested in learning more about the Delano Grape Strike.

- *Delano: The Story Of The California Grape Strike* by John Gregory Dunne: First published in 1967, investigative journalist Dunne does an amazing job of putting you right in the middle of the action. He interviewed Chávez multiple times, rode in the strike caravan, visited worker housing, and interviewed growers. Reading it, I felt like I was in 1960s Delano.

- "Let Them Eat Grapes: The Forgotten Filipinos Who Led A Farmworker Revolution" NPR story: César Chávez may have emerged as the face of the Delano Grape Strike, but Larry Itliong and the AWOC voted to strike a full week before Chávez and the NFWA even got involved.

- UFW website: Whenever I needed to check a specific date or location of the Delano Grape Strike, I'd hop onto the UFW website. They have a lot of great, well-organized information. It's also fun to see how much the union has grown since the NFWA and AWOC combined to form the UFW.

When writing historical fiction, my main goals are to educate and entertain. I hope you've found *United to Strike: A Story of the Delano Grape Workers* both of these.

Photos

Farmworkers pick and pack Malaga grapes in Guasti, California.

Larry Itliong (far left) and César Chávez (far right) unite on the picket line in Delano circa 1965–1966.

Major Events of the Delano Grape Strike

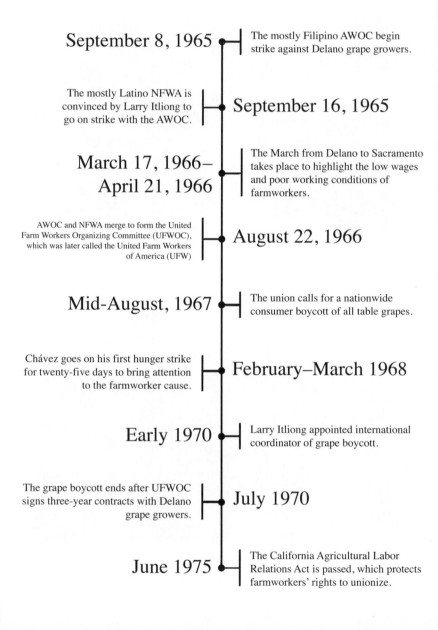

September 8, 1965
The mostly Filipino AWOC begin strike against Delano grape growers.

The mostly Latino NFWA is convinced by Larry Itliong to go on strike with the AWOC.
September 16, 1965

March 17, 1966– April 21, 1966
The March from Delano to Sacramento takes place to highlight the low wages and poor working conditions of farmworkers.

AWOC and NFWA merge to form the United Farm Workers Organizing Committee (UFWOC), which was later called the United Farm Workers of America (UFW)
August 22, 1966

Mid-August, 1967
The union calls for a nationwide consumer boycott of all table grapes.

Chávez goes on his first hunger strike for twenty-five days to bring attention to the farmworker cause.
February–March 1968

Early 1970
Larry Itliong appointed international coordinator of grape boycott.

The grape boycott ends after UFWOC signs three-year contracts with Delano grape growers.
July 1970

June 1975
The California Agricultural Labor Relations Act is passed, which protects farmworkers' rights to unionize.

About the Author

Molly Zenk was born in Minnesota, grew up in Florida, and lived briefly in Tennessee before settling in Colorado. She is married to a mathematician/software engineer who complains there is not enough math or information about him in her author bio. They live in Arvada, Colorado, with their three daughters.

About the Consultant

L. MSP Burns is an Associate Professor in Asian American Studies at UCLA.

About the Illustrator

Eric Freeberg has illustrated over twenty-five books for children, and has created work for magazines and ad campaigns. He was a winner of the 2010 London Book Fair's Children's Illustration Competition; the 2010 Holbein Prize for Fantasy Art, International Illustration Competition, Japan Illustrators' Association; Runner-Up, 2013 SCBWI Magazine Merit Award; Honorable Mention, 2009 SCBWI Don Freeman Portfolio Competition; and 2nd Prize, 2009 Clymer Museum's Annual Illustration Invitational. He was also a winner of the Elizabeth Greenshields Foundation Award.